THE CHRONICLES OF CORK

The Quest for the Book of Light

Aaron McBride & Alton McBride

Portions of this book were developed with the assistance of artificial intelligence tools, under the direction, authorship, and editorial control of the authors.

Book cover design by Aaron McBride, with the assistance of artificial intelligence tools.

ISBN: 979-8-9997020-2-9

First edition.

Printed in the United States of America.

This book is dedicated to the journey shared—
where imagination is trusted,
the Light is sought,
and stories are passed from one generation to the next.

Content

Chapter 1: The Beginning of the End....1

Chapter 2: The Secret Key and the Strange Message.....7

Chapter 3: Static....13

Chapter 4: If You Can Hear....19

Chapter 5: Low Fuel....25

Chapter 6: The Quiet After....31

Chapter 7: The Oasis....39

Chapter 8: Whispers in the Night....45

Chapter 9: The Unfinished Goodbye....51

Chapter 10: Before First Light....55

Chapter 11: The Cost of Knowing....61

Chapter 12: The Hunted....67

Chapter 13: After the Wreck....75

Chapter 14: Shared Light....83

Chapter 15: By What is Marked....89

Chapter 16: A Place Prepared....97

Chapter 17: The Refuge....101

Chapter 18: Stand Tall....109

Chapter 19: Before the Answers....115

Chapter 20: What Has Been Carried..........................123

Chapter 21: Between Belief and Belonging..................129

Chapter 22: The Burning Questions...........................137

Chapter 23: When Darkness is Named........................147

Chapter 24: Where Truth Stands.................................157

Chapter 25: The Table of Trust...................................161

Chapter 26: The Weight of Truth................................169

Chapter 27: The Dream..181

Chapter 28: Awakening..191

Chapter 29: Flight to the Inner Refuge........................197

Chapter 30: Where Silence Gathers...........................207

Chapter 31: The Book of Light....................................215

Chapter 32: After the Light...225

Chapter 33: What Only the Creator Could Do...........231

Chapter 1
The Beginning of the End

The same vision haunted Cork every night.

Even years later, it always began the same way—with sound. Screaming. Running. A city tearing itself apart.

He had been eleven when it happened.

Cork woke to shouting in the street below the apartment. Not the ordinary kind—not neighbors arguing or a television turned too loud. This was panic, sharp and wild, the kind that sank into his bones before his mind could catch up.

He stumbled out of bed and went to the window.

Across the street, the apartment building exploded.

One moment it stood there as it always had. The next, fire tore through its center and burst outward, swallowing windows, walls, and people whole. Flames clawed at the night sky as glass and concrete rained down.

People ran screaming. Some were on fire. Some tripped and fell. Some didn't move again.

Cork stared, frozen.

His eleven-year-old mind refused to understand what his eyes were seeing. It felt unreal, like the world had slipped sideways without warning. Nothing in his life—no lesson, no warning, no nightmare—had prepared him for this.

His chest locked tight, as if the air itself had turned solid. He tried to scream, but the sound never came. He tried to move, but his legs wouldn't answer. His hands trembled uselessly at his sides.

Somewhere deep inside, a voice insisted this couldn't be happening. Buildings didn't explode. People didn't burn. The world didn't simply break apart in front of you.

But it had.

All Cork could do was stand there, frozen, as everything he knew shattered in front of him.

A loud knock slammed into his bedroom door.

"CORK! Are you in there, son?"

His dad's voice cut through the chaos. Cork swallowed hard and forced out a small, shaking answer. "Yes."

The door burst open.

Dad crossed the room in seconds and scooped him into his arms, holding him tight against his chest. An arm locked around Cork's back. His heart was pounding—fast, but steady—and when Cork's ear pressed against his chest, the sound of it filled his head. Each beat landed strong and sure, cutting through the screaming outside, through the distant explosions, through the terror clawing at his thoughts.

The world beyond his father's arms was coming apart, but here—right here—there was rhythm. There was life. As long as that heart kept beating beneath his ear, Cork knew he was still alive.

The fear didn't disappear, but it loosened its grip.

As long as his dad was holding him, he was safe.

"I've got you," Dad said. "Daddy's got you. I'm getting you somewhere safe."

Another blast shook the building.

Dad didn't hesitate. Carrying Cork, he rushed into the hallway. Boots pounded against the floor as the lights flickered. He ducked into the coat closet near the front door and pulled them inside, shutting the door behind them. Dad turned, pressing himself between Cork and the thin wood, his body a shield.

The closet was small and dark. Coats pressed in around them, and the air smelled of dust and old fabric. Cork could hear their breathing. His heart raced, trying to keep up with his father's.

"Where's Mom?" Cork whispered.

Dad's arms tightened.

"She's... she's in a safe place," he said quietly. "Right now, Cork, we need to worry about us."

They stood there, barely breathing.

"Son," Dad whispered, "when I open this door, we may need to run. If the way is clear, we go for the rubble across the street. They won't be searching there for survivors. We're going to—"

The front door exploded.

Dust rained from the ceiling. Cork's ears rang. Heavy boots thundered into the apartment. Voices barked orders. Furniture crashed. Someone ran up the stairs, the floorboards creaking under their weight.

Cork clung to his dad as the ceiling shook. Dad pulled him tighter, one arm firm around his chest. His other hand covered Cork's mouth—not rough, but urgent—holding him still. No sound. Be quiet. Trust me. The message was clear without words.

Minutes passed. Or maybe longer. Time stretched until it felt like they had always been hiding in that closet.

Then everything went quiet.

Cork let out a slow breath.

A thin beam of light crept beneath the crack of the door.

Dad rested a hand on Cork's shoulder and gave it a reassuring squeeze. *I will protect you.*

The doorknob began to turn.

Light spilled into the closet, cutting through the darkness. They pressed deeper into the coats, into the last scraps of shadow.

Then a voice crackled over a radio.

"All units, report back to the convoy. Neighborhood is clear. All citizens have been captured or eliminated."

The light vanished.

Footsteps retreated. The front door slammed shut.

When Dad was sure they were alone, he pulled Cork against his chest so tightly it knocked the breath from him. Then he knelt and held Cork's face in his hands.

"I don't know what's happening," Dad said, his voice breaking. "I don't know who those men were or what they wanted. But I promise you—I will do everything I can to protect you."

Tears streamed down his face.

"I love you."

Cork looked into his father's eyes and understood something he hadn't before.

Whatever had just happened...

His mom wasn't coming back.

Chapter 2
The Secret Key and the Strange Message

Morning came quietly.
Too quietly.

Cork woke on the floor of the apartment with his jacket folded beneath his head and his dad sitting against the wall nearby. For a moment, he forgot where he was.

Then the smell of smoke found him.

It hung in the air—thick and bitter—as if the city itself were holding its breath. His throat felt dry. His eyes burned. Somewhere far away, metal groaned and settled as damaged structures finally gave way.

The world hadn't ended.
It felt like it had.

His dad noticed him stir and shifted closer. "You okay, Cork?" he asked softly.

Cork nodded, even though his chest felt tight and hollow at the same time. A dull ache throbbed behind his eyes, like his head was reminding him how close he'd come to breaking.

The apartment looked wrong in the daylight.

Drawers had been yanked from the dresser and dumped across the floor. Couch cushions lay ripped open, their stuffing scattered like snow. Chairs were overturned. The front door hung crooked on its hinges, sunlight spilling through the shattered frame.

They hadn't just destroyed things.
They had searched.

Cork stood and made his way down the hall toward his room. Every step felt heavier than it should have, as if the floor resisted him. He wanted to stay close to his dad, but something pulled him forward—something that needed to be faced.

His bedroom was worse.

Clothes were strewn everywhere. His desk lay on its side. Books were torn open, their pages bent and ripped as if someone had been in a hurry—or angry.

None of it made sense.

He didn't own anything valuable. No money. No secrets. Just school clothes, a few old toys, and things that only mattered to him.

So what were they looking for?

Cork grabbed an old duffle bag from the closet and dropped it onto the bed. His hands shook as he began stuffing clothes inside—shirts, socks, anything he could reach. Dad had said they couldn't stay. Not here. Not anymore. If they were leaving soon, he needed to be ready.

As he stepped back, his foot crunched against something sharp.

He froze.

Slowly, he looked down.

The frame of their family photo lay shattered at his feet.

The glass had splintered into a thousand pieces, but the picture itself was still intact. His mom smiled up at him from the photograph, her arm wrapped around Dad, Cork standing between them.

His chest tightened.

He knelt and carefully brushed the broken glass aside. A tear slipped free and splashed onto the floor beside the picture. Then another.

Mom was gone.

He knew it now in a way he hadn't let himself know before.

Cork slid the photo into his pocket. As he reached for his favorite hoodie, something caught his eye beneath the bed.

A folded piece of paper.

He frowned and reached for it.

As he unfolded the paper, a small round piece of metal slipped free and clanged against the floor. Cork picked it up and studied it closely.

The disc was thin—about the thickness of a trading card —and roughly the size of a silver dollar. Strange symbols were carved into its surface, worn but deliberate, as if they belonged to an ancient language. Along its edge were small teeth, like part of a gear.

A chill ran down his spine.

Maybe this is what they were searching for.

Cork grabbed the paper the disc had fallen from and read the handwritten words:

The Kingdom is like a treasure hidden in a field, and when a man has found it, he hides, returns home and sells all that he has to purchase the field.

MT 13:44

His thoughts raced.

He didn't know how he knew it, but the weight of the disc in his hand made one thing feel certain.

This wasn't just a message.

There was something more to it.

A key to what, he couldn't say.

Before he could think any further, his dad's voice called up the stairs. "Cork, it's time. We need to go."

He hesitated, the disc warm in his palm. He almost called back—almost asked what it meant, whether his dad recognized the symbols, whether he knew why it had been hidden in Cork's room.

Instead, Cork closed his fingers around the disc and slipped it into his pocket.

Dad stood in the doorway when Cork turned around. He hadn't said anything yet—just watched him, one hand resting against the frame as if holding himself upright. When their eyes met, something tightened in Cork's throat. The disc felt heavier in his pocket, and for a moment he wondered if his dad could tell he was hiding something.

Dad crossed the room and set his hands on Cork's shoulders, searching his face. His eyes looked tired, but steady.

Then he pulled Cork into a quiet hug—firm and sure—like he was reminding him that no matter what they had lost, he wasn't alone.

"You did good, son," Dad said softly. "We'll figure the rest out together."

Cork slung the duffle bag over his shoulder, grabbed the old stuffed rabbit from his bed, and took one last look at his room.

Then he turned and ran down the stairs, leaving his childhood behind.

Chapter 3
Static

The city looked like it had been drained of life.

Cork rode in silence beside his dad as the old pickup rolled through streets that were usually loud even before sunrise. Out here in the desert, mornings belonged to workers and delivery trucks and blinking signs that never really went dark.

Now the signs were dead.

Towering billboards and half-lit marquees leaned over the road. A giant neon crown—once bright enough to paint the clouds—hung dark and crooked, its tubing shattered into jagged lines. Palm trees along the boulevard were scorched at the tips, their fronds hanging limp.

Heat already shimmered over the asphalt, bending the air.

Cars sat abandoned at strange angles, doors left open,

some with alarms chirping weakly until the batteries died. Wind pushed trash and paper cups in slow spirals across empty intersections. In the distance, smoke rose in thin columns, dark against a sky far too blue for what had happened.

Cork kept waiting to see people.
Kept waiting to hear sirens.

But the only sounds were the engine, the rattle of something loose in the truck bed, and the soft hiss of tires rolling over sand blown across the road.

Dad's hands stayed locked on the steering wheel.

The tight line of his jaw said he was holding something together—maybe planning, maybe praying, maybe refusing to fall apart. He checked the rearview mirror every few minutes, like he expected someone to appear behind them.

Cork leaned back in the seat and held the stuffed rabbit against his chest. The duffle bag rested between his feet. Every bump in the road pressed the disc in his pocket against his leg, a quiet reminder that it was still there.

"Where are we going?" Cork asked. His voice sounded small in the quiet cab.

Dad kept his eyes on the road. "Out."

"Out where?"

The truck passed a row of darkened storefronts. One window bore a long crack like a lightning bolt. Another had words scrawled inside in lipstick: **HELP ME**.

Dad swallowed. "Somewhere we can breathe," he said

finally. “Somewhere they won’t look first.”

“They’re still here?”

His grip tightened on the wheel. “I don’t know.”

That should have helped.
It didn’t.

Cork stared toward the edge of the city, where buildings thinned and sand and scrub crept closer to the road. Beyond the last broken lights, the land opened wide and empty.

“Why didn’t anyone help?” he asked.

Dad’s throat moved like he’d swallowed something too big. “They hit fast,” he said. “Too fast.”

Cork wanted to ask more—who they were, what they wanted, where his mom was—but the questions piled up until they felt too heavy to lift.

Dad reached for the radio.

Static filled the cab.

He turned the dial. The noise shifted, rising and falling, but never became words. Another station. More static. He tapped the radio face like it might wake up.

Nothing.

Cork listened anyway, hoping the noise might turn into an answer if he listened hard enough.

Dad turned the volume down. “It’s too early,” he muttered, though Cork wasn’t sure what that meant.

They drove on.

The city fell behind them, and the desert took over. The road stretched ahead in a straight line that seemed to point toward the edge of the world. Sunlight poured down, bright and unforgiving. Heat waves danced above the hood.

The farther they went, the emptier it became.

No cars passed them.
No planes crossed the sky.

Just open desert and a thin ribbon of highway.

Dad tried the radio again.

Static.

A flicker of sound slipped through for half a second—a voice, maybe, or maybe imagination—and then vanished.

"Did you hear that?" Cork asked.

Dad's eyes sharpened. He turned the dial slowly, carefully, as if the right frequency might break if touched wrong.

Static.

Then—

A long, piercing tone cut through the noise.

Cork's stomach dropped.

The emergency signal.

Dad's hand froze on the knob.

The tone sounded again, followed by a shift in the static, thinner now, strained. A voice tried to push through.

“This is—” it crackled, uneven, breathless. “This is an emergency—broadcast—if you can hear—”

The signal wavered.

“—repeat—stay off—roads—do not—”

Dad leaned closer, eyes wide.

The voice vanished.

Static roared back in.

Dad tapped the dashboard once, light but urgent. “Come on,” he whispered.

The emergency tone sounded one last time.

Then, through the noise, the voice returned—faint, fractured, fighting to be heard.

“—Circle... of One... approaching—”

Chapter 4
If You Can Hear

Dad eased the truck onto the shoulder and let it roll to a stop. The engine idled, ticking and rattling as if trying to catch its breath. Heat pressed in through the open windows, carrying the dry smell of dust and burned metal.

Neither of them spoke.

The silence felt heavier now that they had stopped. While they were moving, the road had given them something to focus on. Sitting still let everything else rush in—questions mostly, sharp and insistent. A dull pressure settled behind Cork's eyes, not quite pain, just enough to make it hard to think straight.

The desert stretched out on both sides of the road, flat and endless, broken only by scrub brush and the occasional telephone pole marching toward the horizon. Heat shimmered above the pavement. Behind them, the city crouched low and quiet, its dark signs and shattered lights already beginning to feel far away.

Dad leaned forward and turned the radio up.

Static filled the cab, loud and angry. He turned the dial slowly, carefully, as if the sound might shatter if he moved too fast.

The emergency tone cut in—sharp and piercing—then vanished, leaving the cab feeling suddenly too small.

Cork's stomach tightened. He pressed his palm against his thigh, grounding himself, while the pressure behind his eyes rose and fell with the uneven rhythm of the radio.

The tone sounded again, longer this time. The static thinned just enough for voices to push through.

"This is—" a voice crackled, strained and breathless. Something slammed in the background. Another voice shouted, muffled and urgent. "—emergency broadcast—if you can hear—"

The signal wavered. A siren wailed somewhere far away, then cut off abruptly.

"—multiple cities—no confirmed command—" the voice continued, breaking apart. Someone coughed violently near the microphone. "—stay off major roads—repeat—stay—"

The transmission dissolved back into noise.

Dad's jaw tightened. For a brief moment, his eyes closed —just long enough to brace himself. He reached for the volume knob, then stopped, as if touching it again might make things worse.

The emergency tone pierced the static once more.

A different voice came through this time—higher, panicked.

"—Circle of One—approaching—if you can hear this, shelter—do not—"

A loud crash echoed through the broadcast, followed by shouting. The voice disappeared.

Static roared back, swallowing the last echoes and leaving only noise and unanswered warnings behind.

Cork swallowed. His throat felt dry, tight. "Dad?"

Dad didn't answer right away. His eyes stayed fixed on the dashboard, on the radio that refused to tell them everything they needed to know.

"What does that mean?" Cork asked. "The Circle of One?"

Dad exhaled slowly. "It means we weren't wrong to leave." His voice stayed steady, but his shoulders remained tense.

That wasn't an answer.

"Are they close?"

Dad shook his head. "I don't know."

"But you've heard of them." It wasn't a question.

Dad's hands rested on the steering wheel, knuckles pale. The muscles in his forearms were tight, like he was holding back more than words. "I've heard rumors," he said. "Warnings. Things people didn't want to take seriously."

"Like what?"

Dad glanced at Cork, just for a second. Something heavy sat in his eyes—fear, maybe, or regret. "Like the kind of trouble that doesn't announce itself until it's already too late."

The radio crackled again. Dad leaned closer, hopeful despite himself.

"This is an emergency—" the first voice returned, faint and rushed. "—command structure compromised—resources limited—if you can hear—"

A sharp squeal of feedback cut the voice off mid-sentence.

Silence.

The kind that rang louder than the static.

Dad turned the radio down, but not off. The static lingered low and restless, as if waiting for the wrong moment to surge back.

Cork hugged the stuffed rabbit tighter against his chest. Its worn fur was warm from his hands, familiar in a way nothing else was anymore. The light outside felt too sharp, like his eyes couldn't quite keep up with everything that was happening.

"So what do we do?" Cork asked.

Dad started the truck. The engine's growl felt loud in the stillness. "We keep moving," he said. "Listening won't keep us safe."

He checked the mirrors, then pulled back onto the road.

As the truck picked up speed, Cork looked back once at the quiet stretch of desert shoulder where they had stopped to listen.

The radio stayed silent.

And that scared him more than anything it had said.

Chapter 5
Low Fuel

The fuel needle hovered just above empty.

Dad slowed as another gas station slid past on their right, its pumps wrapped in yellow tape. A piece of cardboard had been stapled to the door, thick black letters scrawled across it: **OUT OF FUEL**. The sign flapped weakly in the heat.

"That's the third one," Cork said.

Dad nodded but didn't answer. His eyes stayed on the road, scanning ahead like he was weighing options they couldn't afford.

They passed a fourth station a mile later. Its windows were boarded, the pumps dragged sideways, hoses torn loose. No sign this time. Just emptiness.

When the next station appeared, Dad slowed again.

It was small—two pumps, a low building with sun-faded lettering, and a narrow awning that cast a thin strip of shade. No tape. No cardboard sign. One pump stood upright, its screen dark but intact.

Dad eased into the lot and shut off the engine.

“Stay here,” he said.

He reached into the truck bed, grabbed the old red gas can, hesitated, then picked it up. “Lock the doors.”

Cork did.

Dad crossed the lot and pushed through the door, the bell chiming once before falling silent.

Cork stayed in the truck and watched.

The station felt exposed. Open desert on three sides. The road stretching away in both directions, nowhere to hide. Heat shimmered off the pavement, blurring the edges of everything.

Two other vehicles sat near the pumps—an SUV with tinted windows and a dented sedan missing a headlight. No movement inside either one.

Cork shifted in his seat. The disc pressed against his leg, a small, solid weight that felt heavier than it should have. He slid his hand into his pocket just enough to touch it.

The metal felt cool.

For a moment, the symbols came back to him—the sharp angles of the triangle, the strange letters that looked familiar without making sense. Lines connected them, precise and deliberate, like they were meant to point somewhere.

He pushed the disc deeper into his pocket and pressed his hand flat against the fabric, as if that might keep it hidden.

Inside the station, Dad stood at the counter. The attendant was thin, dark circles under his eyes, a week's worth of stubble shadowing his jaw. He didn't smile. He didn't frown. He just watched.

Dad said something Cork couldn't hear.

The attendant's eyes flicked past him—past the counter—toward the window.

Toward Cork.

This time, the look didn't pass.

The attendant stared openly, his expression flat and unreadable, as if measuring something Cork didn't understand. The seconds stretched. Heat shimmered outside the glass. Cork stared straight ahead, every instinct screaming not to move, not to look back.

When the attendant finally turned away, the tension didn't leave with him.

The bell chimed again as someone stepped out from the back room. Another man, older and heavier, his shirt stained with oil. He leaned against the wall and crossed his arms.

Dad lifted the gas can.

The attendant said something short and sharp.

Dad replied, slower this time.

The attendant shook his head.

Cork's shoulders tightened. He gripped the stuffed rabbit so hard his fingers sank into the worn fabric.

The attendant leaned closer to the counter, his mouth moving again. The older man shifted his weight.

Dad said something Cork couldn't hear, but his shoulders stiffened.

After a long moment, the attendant reached under the counter. He pulled out a small stack of bills, tapped them once against the surface, then pushed them back as if they didn't mean much anymore.

Dad shook his head.

The attendant's lips pressed together. He lifted a finger and said something that made Dad pause.

Dad nodded once.

The older man uncrossed his arms.

A few minutes later, Dad came back outside. He didn't look at Cork as he passed the truck. He went straight to the pump and set the gas can down.

The pump coughed once before fuel began to flow.

Dad kept his back to the building as the numbers ticked upward. The sound of liquid filling the can seemed too loud in the open lot.

Cork watched the door.

The attendant stood just inside, arms resting on the counter, eyes never leaving them.

Dad filled the can halfway, shut it off, then moved to the truck and fueled directly.

When he finished, he tightened the cap, lifted the can, and walked back.

"Everything okay?" Cork asked through the closed window.

Dad nodded. "We're fine."

But his jaw stayed tight.

Dad stowed the gas can in the bed and climbed in, starting the engine immediately.

As they pulled away, Cork glanced back.

The attendant was still watching.

The station shrank behind them, swallowed by heat and distance. The fuel needle climbed just enough to make Cork breathe again.

Dad didn't speak until the road stretched empty in front of them.

"We won't stop again unless we have to," he said.

Cork nodded.

His hand drifted to his pocket.

The disc was still there.

And for the first time, Cork wondered who else might be looking for it.

Chapter 6
The Quiet After

The road began to change.

The desert didn't disappear, but it stopped being flat. Sand gave way to hard-packed earth and red stone that rose in wide shelves beside the highway. Farther out, cliffs and mesas lifted from the ground like the world had folded itself into layers. Shadows pooled in the cracks and canyons, dark even under the relentless sun.

Dad drove with both hands on the wheel.

The truck's engine hummed steady, but everything else felt too quiet—like the air itself was listening.

They didn't pass another car for a long time.

The gas station was already gone behind them, swallowed by heat and distance, but the feeling of eyes on Cork's back wouldn't fade. Every bend in the road made him expect movement in the mirror. A dark SUV. A line of vehicles. Someone following.

Dad checked the rear-view mirror frequently.

Not frantic. Just often enough to be noticed.

The fuel needle sat higher now—not full, but better. It should have brought relief.

It didn't.

The stuffed rabbit rested in Cork's lap. He ran his thumb along one torn ear, back and forth, the way he used to when sleep wouldn't come.

Dad kept the radio off.

Cork waited for the familiar rush of static, for the emergency tone, for any voice to break the silence. But the dashboard stayed dark, the knobs untouched.

"Why aren't you turning it on?" Cork asked.

Dad kept his eyes on the road. "Because it doesn't help."

"It told us something."

"It told us enough."

The words landed like a closed door.

The road climbed gradually. The air outside looked thinner somehow, brighter. The sky stretched wide and hard, the kind of blue that made the world feel exposed.

They passed a road sign riddled with bullet holes. The metal was bent, the lettering half peeled away.

Dad slowed just long enough to read what remained.

Then he sped up.

The disc pressed against Cork's leg.

He didn't reach for it this time. He just felt it there—a secret with weight.

Questions crowded in, sharp and restless.

Why had it been in his room?
Why hidden beneath the picture?
Why would soldiers tear their home apart looking for something small enough to fit in a pocket?

And why did it feel like it had been waiting?

If it mattered that much, why leave a message instead of an answer?

Cork swallowed and glanced at Dad.

His face looked older than it had the day before. The lines around his eyes seemed deeper, carved by the last forty-eight hours.

"Dad."

Dad didn't answer right away, but he did glance over.

The questions pressed closer—where they were really going, what he'd said to the man at the station, what he wasn't saying now.

Instead, Cork asked something smaller. Safer.

"How far can we go now?"

Dad nodded once, like he'd been waiting for that one. "Farther," he said. "Not forever. But farther."

"Is that enough?"

Dad's mouth tightened. "It has to be."

They drove in silence again.

The land kept changing. Low hills became long ridges. Ridges rose into plateaus. In the distance, tall rock formations stood like watchmen, striped in red and tan and shadow. The sun hammered down, but the wind shifted at higher ground, cooler in short bursts through the cracked windows.

A hawk circled overhead.

Its shadow slid across the road and vanished beneath the truck.

Cork flinched anyway.

Dad noticed. His grip tightened, then relaxed. "We're okay," he said—but it sounded less like a promise than something he needed to believe.

The truck hit a rough patch. The rabbit bounced against Cork's stomach.

The disc shifted in his pocket.

He pressed his hand flat against the fabric, holding it in place.

Dad's eyes flicked to the movement.

For a moment, it felt like he might say something.

He didn't.

That silence rang louder than the radio ever had.

The road dipped into a shallow valley where rock walls rose on both sides. The shadows there were deeper, cooler. The sun couldn't reach the bottom of the cuts in the stone.

Dad eased off the gas.

"What?" Cork asked.

Dad leaned forward slightly, eyes narrowing.

Up ahead, something lay on the shoulder—a shredded tire, empty, placed too neatly to be chance.

Then more appeared.

A fallen traffic cone.
A splintered piece of pallet.
Scraps that didn't belong on a lonely stretch of road.

Dad's jaw tightened.

He didn't slow.

He didn't stop.

They passed the debris and kept going.

Only when the valley opened back into sunlight did Dad finally speak.

"People do desperate things," he said quietly.

Cork looked at him. "Were they trying to make us stop?"

Dad's throat moved. "Maybe."

Cork's skin prickled.
The world wasn't just broken.

It was hungry.

He looked down at the rabbit in his lap and tried to picture his mom's face the way it used to be—warm, smiling, safe.

The image wouldn't hold.

That familiar pressure settled behind his eyes again. Not

pain. Just the sense of being stretched too thin.

"Dad," Cork said softly. "Do you think... do you think we'll ever go home?"

Dad didn't answer.

The truck kept moving, tires singing over the road.

Then, finally, he spoke—careful, measured, like each word cost him something.

"I don't know."

It wasn't the answer Cork wanted.

But it was the first time he believed him completely.

The sun slid lower, and the rock formations ahead began to glow along their edges. Reds deepened. Shadows lengthened.

Dad glanced toward the horizon. "We'll need to find a place before dark."

"Another station?"

Dad shook his head. "Not a station."

He hesitated.

"There's a place," he said slowly. "People who still... still open their doors sometimes."

Cork waited.

Dad didn't say the name.

Not yet.

But something in his voice—quieter, steadier—made something inside Cork lift, just a little.

As the truck climbed toward the next ridge, Cork felt the disc in his pocket again.

Heavy.
Hidden.
Waiting.

And as the sky dimmed at the edges, he wondered whether it was leading them toward that place—

Or leading something toward them.

Chapter 7
The Oasis

They reached it just before the light began to fail.

From the road, it didn't look like much. A low, square building half-buried in sand and scrub, its paint bleached nearly the same color as the desert around it. The sign out front leaned at an angle, one corner snapped loose so it creaked softly in the wind.

THE OASIS

The words were faded, the letters chipped and uneven, like they'd been repainted more than once and never quite the same way twice.

Dad slowed the truck long before they pulled in.

Dim light glowed inside, covered with cloth and cardboard so it wouldn't spill far into the open desert. A figure moved near the entrance, then stopped. Another shape appeared behind it. They watched the truck for a long moment before anyone came closer.

Dad shut off the engine but didn't open the door.

They waited.

Finally, a man stepped forward, one hand raised—not in greeting, but in warning. He was thin, his clothes dusty and worn, his eyes always moving.

"State your business," he called.

"We're passing through," Dad said through the open window. "Just looking for a place to rest. We won't stay long."

The man studied Dad's face, then glanced at Cork.

"Anyone follow you?"

"No."

The man hesitated, then nodded once. "Before dark only," he said. "You leave at first light."

The door opened.

Inside, the air was cooler, thick with dust and the smell of old wood and oil. Cork knew at once what the building had been—not because anyone said it, but because of the shape of the room. The way the ceiling lifted higher at one end. The faint outline where something had once hung, removed so completely it left only absence behind.

The pews were gone.

Mattresses and blankets covered the floor. People sat in small clusters, speaking in low voices or not speaking at all. Children clung to parents. Someone coughed. Someone cried quietly behind a stack of boxes.

A cracked mural stretched across the far wall. Whatever it had once shown was scraped away in places, leaving scars where something meaningful had stood.

Dad rested a hand on Cork's shoulder.

"We'll stay out of the way," he said to the man.

"That's best," the man replied. "Questions make people nervous."

As they moved deeper inside, Cork listened.

"...not just here," someone whispered nearby. "Europe first. Then the coasts."

"...took the broadcast towers. Relay stations. Anything that carried a message too far."

"...leaders vanished overnight. Not dead. Gone."

"...they don't want chaos. They want quiet."

The fragments overlapped, unfinished, but together they formed something heavy in Cork's chest.

It didn't sound like one city. Not the way people were talking. The places they mentioned were too far apart, the fear too practiced, like they'd been carrying it longer than just a day or two.

Cork didn't know how far it went. He didn't know how big it was.

But whatever had happened to their city hadn't stayed there.

Dad spoke quietly with an older woman near the wall. Her face was lined and tired, her voice steady.

"They hit places like this early," she said. "Anywhere people gathered for something bigger than themselves."

"For faith?" Dad asked.

She shrugged. "For resistance."

Nearby, a man laughed softly—not kindly.

"Resistance," he said. "That's what they call it when you won't fall in line."

Someone else leaned in. "The Circle of One isn't against people being happy," she said. "They let you live your life. Work. Eat. Want things. They only come when you won't stop telling others there's something higher."

"They promise peace," another voice added. "Unity. No more division."

"And if you agree?" Cork asked before he could stop himself.

The room went quiet.

A few heads turned.

The man who had laughed studied him for a long moment. "Then they leave you alone," he said. "Mostly."

Dad's hand tightened on Cork's shoulder.

"Until you say the wrong thing," someone muttered.

"Or believe the wrong thing," another voice added.

The word *Creator* drifted through the room like something dangerous.

Dad stiffened.

A woman shook her head. "If the Creator was still watching," she said, "this wouldn't have happened."

No one answered her.

Cork thought of his mom. The way she used to talk about truth like it mattered more than comfort. The way belief never sounded fragile when she spoke of it.

"They're not after everyone," someone said quietly. "Just the ones who won't stop resisting. The ones who won't trade truth for safety."

Dad closed his eyes for a brief moment.

Later, as the light outside faded from gold to purple to gray, Cork and Dad sat against the wall, backs pressed to cool stone. The stuffed rabbit rested in Cork's lap. The disc pressed against his leg.

"This place won't last," the older woman said as she passed them. "None of them do."

"Where do people go?" Cork asked.

She hesitated. "Somewhere deeper," she said. "Somewhere quieter."

Then she leaned closer. "If you're smart, you don't stay here long."

Outside, the wind picked up, rattling the loose sign.

THE OASIS creaked in the dark.

Cork looked at Dad. He stared at the floor, jaw tight, like he was holding something back.

"Dad," Cork whispered.

Dad didn't answer.

But as the lights dimmed further and the room settled into uneasy sleep, something became suddenly clear.

This place wasn't meant to save anyone.

Chapter 8
Whispers in the Night

The lights inside the Oasis dimmed gradually, one by one, until the room settled into a low amber glow that barely reached the corners. Someone hung a blanket dimming the lantern light near the back wall, muting it further. Shadows stretched long across the floor, broken only by the slow movement of people trying to find rest.

Bodies grew still.
The room did not truly sleep.

Cork and Dad found a place along the wall where the stone felt cool even through their clothes. Dad spread a thin blanket on the floor, and Cork curled against it, the stuffed rabbit tucked beneath his arm. His muscles ached with the kind of exhaustion that should have brought sleep easily.

It didn't.

Whispers continued in the darkness. Low voices slipped through the room, rising and falling like wind through broken windows.

"...they wouldn't have come if we hadn't resisted."

"...said they could keep the power on, if we just stopped..."

"...unity is better than chaos. Isn't it?"

Cork shut his eyes and tried to imagine his bed back home. The smell of the sheets. The hum of the old fan by the window. But every time he started to drift, another voice pulled him back.

Dad lay beside him on his back, one arm folded across his chest, the other resting near Cork's shoulder. His breathing was slow. Measured.

Too measured.

Cork watched the rise and fall of his chest and tried to match it, the way he used to when sleep wouldn't come. Back then, it always worked. Dad's steady breathing meant everything was fine.

Tonight, it felt like something was being held back.

Dad wasn't asleep either.

A voice nearby cut through the murmurs, sharper than the rest. "You can't fight an idea," a man said. "That's what they keep telling us. You either join it, or you get crushed by it."

Another voice answered, softer. "They say belief divides people. That truth caused all of this."

A pause followed.

"Maybe peace matters more than being right."

The words settled heavily into the room.

Dad shifted beside Cork. Just enough to be noticed.

A woman near the center let out a tired laugh. “They don’t stop you from wanting things,” she said. “You can still eat, work, build a life. They just don’t want anyone telling others there’s something higher than the One.”

“Because that makes people dangerous,” someone replied.

Silence followed again. Thicker this time.

Cork rolled onto his side. The stone wall pressed cold against his shoulder blade. He welcomed the chill. It was simple. It didn’t argue or ask him to choose. His chest felt tight, like he’d been holding his breath without noticing.

The whispers blurred together until they sounded like one long argument he didn’t want to hear anymore.

The rabbit’s ear brushed his chin as he shifted. His hand slipped into his pocket out of habit—

—and touched paper.

He froze.

Carefully, slowly, Cork pulled the folded page free, shielding it with his body so the dim light wouldn’t catch it. The paper was creased now, softened from being handled.

Familiar.

He unfolded it just enough to read.

The Kingdom is like a treasure hidden in a field...

He read the words once.
Then again.

They didn't explain anything. They didn't tell him what to do or where to go. They didn't promise safety or peace.

But they didn't sound afraid either.

Cork thought of the voices behind him—of unity and comfort and survival. Of how reasonable it all sounded when someone was tired and scared and wanted the noise to stop.

The words on the paper didn't argue back.

They just waited.

Movement beside him made his muscles tense. Somewhere across the room, a child whimpered in their sleep, calling out to someone who didn't answer. An older man murmured a prayer under his breath, too quiet to make out.

Then Dad turned onto his side, facing Cork. His eyes were open, catching what little light remained.

"You okay?" Dad whispered.

Cork nodded quickly and folded the paper, sliding it back into his pocket. His throat felt tight, like he'd done something wrong without knowing why.

"Try to sleep," Dad said. His voice was gentle, but strained.

"I am," Cork whispered back.

Dad watched him for another moment, then looked

away, staring up at the ceiling as if it might offer answers if he waited long enough.

The room grew quieter as the night wore on. Even the whispers seemed to tire. Feet shuffled softly. Someone coughed. Another voice murmured about leaving at first light—about how staying meant being found.

No one argued.

Someone near the door gathered their things quietly and slipped out, careful not to wake anyone.

Cork smoothed the folded paper inside his pocket, running his thumb along its edge.

The words still didn't make sense.

But they didn't feel like a lie.

Outside, the wind brushed against the building, rattling the loose sign again. The Oasis held—fragile, temporary—as the people inside rested in discomfort.

As the dark thinned toward morning, a quiet thought settled in—unfinished, uncomfortable.

Staying here might be easier.

But ease had never felt like the same thing as enough.

Chapter 9
The Unfinished Goodbye

Sleep came in pieces.

Not the kind that rested you, but the kind that pulled Cork under when his body could no longer stay awake. His thoughts blurred, folded in on themselves, and the voices in the room faded into something distant and hollow.

At first, it felt like he was still awake.

He stood in a place that felt familiar but wrong, like a memory he couldn't quite finish. The air was warm—not desert-hot, but soft. The ground beneath his feet wasn't stone or sand. It felt like the old carpet from the living room, worn thin in places from years of pacing and play.

"Cork."

He turned.

She was there.

Not the way he had last seen her. Not afraid. Not hurried. She stood the way she used to when she was waiting for him—arms relaxed at her sides, head tilted slightly, a small smile that meant she was listening.

"Mom?"

The word came out smaller than he expected.

She stepped closer and cupped his face in her hands. Her palms were warm. Real. She smelled like soap and something familiar he couldn't name.

"I know," she said softly. "I know."

Tears burned behind his eyes. "They said—" The words tangled in his throat. "You didn't come back."

She brushed her thumb beneath his eye, catching the tear before it fell. "I didn't leave you," she said. "Not the way you think."

The weight in his chest shifted—not gone, but lighter.

"I was scared," he said.

"Of course you were."

"Dad's scared too."

"I know."

Cork glanced around, unease creeping in. "Is this real?"

She smiled—not sadly, not brightly. Just steady. "For now," she said. "It's enough."

"Why didn't you tell us?" he asked.

Her hands stilled.

“There are things,” she said carefully, “that don’t survive being said too early.”

Cork thought of the voices in the Oasis. The promises. The calm logic. How reasonable it all sounded when people were tired and afraid.

“They say it’s easier if you don’t resist,” he said. “They say peace matters more.”

Her eyes softened, but they didn’t waver. “Easy and safe aren’t the same thing,” she said. “And peace that asks you to let go of truth doesn’t stay peaceful for long.”

He swallowed. “Did it hurt?”

She rested her forehead against his. “Yes.”

The honesty startled him.

“But it mattered,” she continued. “And I would make the same choice again.”

His chest tightened. “I don’t know how,” he said. “I don’t know what I’m supposed to do.”

“You don’t have to,” she said. “Not yet.”

Her hand settled on his shoulder, firm and reassuring. “Just don’t stop listening.”

The space around them began to thin, like mist burned away by light.

“Mom?”

“I’m proud of you,” she said. “For holding what you don’t understand.”

He reached for her, but his fingers passed through

warmth into air.

Cork woke with a sharp breath.

The Oasis was still dark. The room smelled of dust and old stone. Someone nearby shifted in sleep. Dad lay beside him, turned away, his breathing uneven now.

Cork's heart pounded.

For a moment, it was hard to tell where the dream ended and the night began.

He slipped a hand into his pocket and touched the folded paper and the disc. They were still there. Solid. Real.

The words lingered—not spoken now, just felt.

Don't stop listening.

Outside, the wind moved again, rattling the loose sign above the entrance. Metal scraped softly against stone, a restless sound.

Morning wasn't far away.

Chapter 10
Before First Light

Shouting tore through the dark.

Cork jerked awake as voices collided near the entrance of the Oasis—sharp, panicked, angry. A bench scraped across the stone floor. A lantern tipped, its light swinging wildly and throwing jagged shadows against the walls.

“What are you hiding?” someone yelled.

Dad was already moving, pulling Cork to his feet. His heart hammered as they were swept along by bodies pressing toward the noise.

Near the doorway, two men had hold of another, his jacket half torn from his shoulders as he struggled. His words spilled out fast and desperate.

“I didn’t choose it—I swear—”

A hand yanked his collar down.

The room went silent.

Just below the man's collarbone, dark ink curved against his skin. A symbol—circular, closed, its lines smooth and deliberate. Simple. Final.

No one spoke at first.

People leaned in without realizing it. Others took a step back. Someone near the wall crossed themselves, then froze, unsure if that was still allowed. The symbol seemed to pull the room toward it, bending attention, tightening breath.

"He's marked," someone finally whispered.

The word broke whatever fragile stillness remained.

Fear snapped back into motion.

Shouts broke out—some demanding the man be thrown out, others shouting that anyone could be forced to wear a mark.

"They made me," the man cried. "You think I wanted this?"

A fist struck him.

The words stopped.

Dad's hand came down hard on Cork's shoulder. "Eyes down," he said quietly.

Cork did—but the image burned itself into his mind anyway.

The man was dragged toward the door, his heels scraping against stone. The loose sign outside groaned as the door was flung open, spilling cold air and darkness into the room. Then the door slammed shut.

Silence followed.

Heavy.

An older voice cut through it, steady but worn thin. “I warned you,” the caretaker said. His gaze swept the room and settled briefly on Dad and Cork. “You need to leave before first light. We can’t keep anyone safe anymore.”

Murmurs rippled through the space.

“If you’re leaving,” the caretaker continued, “leave now.”

Dad didn’t argue. He grabbed their duffle and nodded toward the side exit. They moved quickly, past people frozen in place, past others scrambling to gather what little they had.

Near the side door, an elderly woman stood watching the chaos with clear, steady eyes. Her hair was silver and pulled back neatly. Her posture was straight despite her years. A worn satchel hung at her side.

“You’re heading out,” she said quietly.

Dad stopped. “We are.”

“Good,” she replied. “Staying costs more than leaving.”

She glanced back into the room—at the whispers, the wary looks, the sudden distance between people. Then she turned and motioned toward the exit. “Not here,” she said under her breath. “Too many ears.”

Outside, the pre-dawn air was cold and sharp. She kept a careful distance until they reached the truck.

Only then did she open her satchel and unfold a hand-drawn map, the paper thick and creased from use. Dark circles and lines covered it.

“Roadblocks here,” she said, tapping several places with a firm finger. “Patrols move, but these don’t. They watch the main highways first.”

Dad leaned closer. “How far is it?”

“Far enough that you’ll have to mean it,” she said. “Too far to wander.”

Her eyes flicked to the truck. “How much fuel?”

“Most of a tank,” Dad said. “And a can.”

She nodded once. “It should get you close. If you’re careful.”

She traced a longer route, circling wide around the marked roads. “This way’s slower,” she said. “But it keeps you out of sight.”

Cork edged closer to Dad. Something in the way she spoke—like she understood the cost—tightened his chest.

She studied Cork then. Really studied him.

“People don’t leave in the dark unless they’re searching for something,” she said quietly. “Most are just running.”

Her gaze returned to Dad. “Your wife believed truth was worth more than safety. We crossed paths once—long enough for me to recognize that kind of conviction.”

Dad’s breath caught.

"You don't forget it," she added.

She folded the map and handed it to him. "My name is Deborah."

"Will you come with us?" Cork asked before he could stop himself.

Deborah smiled—not sadly, not afraid. Just sure. "My road doesn't run the same way as yours," she said. "But you're meant to keep going."

The sky had begun to pale. The desert stretched wide and empty again, waiting.

Dad squeezed Cork's shoulder. "We go now."

The truck rumbled to life. Dad checked the fuel gauge, then unfolded the map across his knee.

They didn't look back.

The Oasis faded into darkness behind them, the loose sign creaking once more in the wind.

"We can make it," Dad said. "If nothing goes wrong."

Cork watched the road narrow into the distance.

And hoped he was right.

Chapter 11
The Cost of Knowing

The truck hummed steadily as the desert slipped past, mile after mile of open land washed in pale morning light. The sky was no longer dark, but the sun had not yet fully risen. Everything felt suspended, as if the world itself were holding its breath.

For a long time, neither of them spoke.

The road stretched straight ahead, no longer boxed in by stone and sand, opening instead into wide, rolling land. Scrub thinned into tall grasses that bent and whispered in the wind. The hard edges of mesas softened into distant rises that seemed to go on forever. Fence posts flicked past in steady rhythm, and the heat eased, carried off by a breeze that smelled faintly of earth instead of dust.

Dad kept both hands on the wheel, his eyes scanning the road, the mirrors, the horizon—everywhere at once. A folded paper map lay open on the seat between them, its edges worn soft, one corner marked with a rough pencil circle Deborah had drawn before they left the Oasis.

Cork shifted in his seat. The worn fabric felt warm against his arms. The stuffed rabbit rested in his lap, its fur matted and familiar. The duffle bag sat between his feet. Every so often, the hard edge of the disc pressed against his leg through his pocket, a quiet reminder of everything he didn't understand.

"Dad?"

Dad didn't look over right away. "Yeah, Cork?"

"I... I dreamed about Mom last night."

Dad's grip tightened on the wheel. The truck drifted slightly before he corrected it. "What about her?" His voice was careful.

Cork kept his eyes on the passing land. "She was standing somewhere bright. Not like the desert—brighter. And she wasn't scared."

Dad swallowed.

"She told me not to be afraid," Cork continued. "She said the truth was worth holding onto, even when it hurt."

Silence settled between them, heavier than before.

"That sounds like her," Dad said quietly.

Cork turned toward him. "Deborah said she knew Mom. Did Mom ever tell you about her?"

Dad shook his head. "No. Your mom didn't talk much about the people she met." After a pause, he added, "She said some things were safer kept small."

Cork frowned. "Do you think she knew more than we did?"

Dad's jaw shifted as if he were weighing the question. "I think," he said carefully, "that your mom saw things more clearly than I wanted to."

He took one hand off the wheel long enough to rub his face. "I thought keeping our heads down would be enough. Thought if we didn't draw attention, we'd be fine."

"But she didn't," Cork said.

"No," Dad replied. "She believed truth mattered more than comfort."

The words stayed with them.

Wind brushed along the side of the truck, rattling faintly at the door. For a moment, it felt like the world was listening. Cork wondered if Mom had ever sat in a moment like this—halfway between safety and danger—knowing there was no turning back.

He picked at a loose thread on his sleeve. "Do you think she knew what would happen?"

Dad was quiet for a long time. The road hummed beneath the tires, steady and unforgiving. "I think she knew there would be a cost," he said at last. "I don't think she knew how high it would be."

His voice dropped. "Sometimes I wonder if I would've tried to stop her... if she'd told me everything."

After a moment, Cork asked, "What about the mark?

The one on that man?"

Dad exhaled slowly. "I've heard of it. Not like that—but whispers. Symbols people were forced to wear. Or chose to wear. It's not always easy to tell the difference."

"Why would someone choose it?"

"Because it promises safety," Dad said. "Or power. Or belonging." He glanced over. "Those promises come with a price."

He hesitated. "And the price isn't always paid by the one who chooses."

The truck rolled on. The road narrowed as it bent between rocky outcroppings. Dad reached down and tapped the fuel gauge once with his finger.

"I thought we'd have farther," he muttered. "I should've planned better."

"You did," Cork said quickly. "Deborah said it would be close."

Dad nodded, but the tension in his shoulders didn't ease.

The needle hovered lower than it should have.

Cork's stomach tightened. "Is something wrong?"

"We're using more than I expected," Dad said. "Wind. Terrain."

He didn't say anything else, but his eyes kept returning to the gauge.

Cork hesitated, then asked, "Dad... are you scared?"

Dad pressed his lips together. For a moment, it seemed like he wouldn't answer.

"Yes," he said quietly.

The word stayed there, simple and heavy.

"But I'm not scared of the road," he added. "I'm scared of failing you."

Cork's chest tightened. "You're not," he said. "You're still here."

Dad nodded once, like he was holding onto that truth with both hands.

Cork leaned his head against the window. The vibration of the road tugged gently at his thoughts. The sun climbed higher, warmth pressing through the glass. His eyelids grew heavy.

"Get some rest," Dad said softly. "I'll wake you if I need you."

Cork nodded, unsure what that might mean.

Sleep came in fragments.

He didn't know how long it had been when the truck jolted.

Cork's eyes flew open as the engine sputtered, then smoothed out again. Dad eased the truck toward the shoulder, gravel crunching beneath the tires.

"What's happening?" Cork asked, his heart pounding.

Dad shifted the truck into park and reached for the door. "We're okay," he said, though his voice was tight. "Fuel gauge just hit empty faster than I like."

He grabbed the gas can from the truck bed and stepped out into the open plains, tall grass bending softly along the shoulder.

Cork watched through the window as Dad twisted the cap loose. The faint smell of fuel drifted in the air.

The road behind them lay empty.

But the silence felt wrong.

And Cork couldn't shake the feeling that stopping—even for a moment—had made them visible.

Chapter 12

The Hunted

Dusk settled slowly across the plains—not with the sudden fall of darkness Cork expected, but like a long breath being released. The sky deepened from pale blue to bruised purple, streaked with thin bands of orange that faded as the sun slipped beyond the low, rolling horizon.

The road felt lonelier now.

Fence lines stretched on either side, posts leaning at tired angles, wire humming faintly as the wind slid through. Tall grass bent and whispered in waves, brushing the edge of the pavement as if it meant to reclaim it. The land was wide—too wide—with nowhere to hide.

Dad drove with both hands tight on the wheel, his gaze fixed far ahead, as though he were reading the land itself instead of the road. The map Deborah had marked lay folded beside him, untouched. Whatever guidance it had offered earlier, he wasn't relying on it now.

They passed an exit ramp leading to a highway. The overhead sign was dark, its reflective paint cracked and peeling.

Dad slowed, but didn't turn.

Cork watched the ramp slip past. "We're not taking that?"

Dad shook his head. "Too visible."

The light dimmed further, the sky pressing low. Dad reached out and twisted a knob near the wheel.

The headlights clicked off.

Cork's heart jumped.

"We'll see enough," Dad said quietly. "Trust me."

The road ahead became a darker ribbon, barely visible against the grass. Cork leaned forward, straining his eyes. Every shadow felt like movement. Every dip in the land threatened to swallow them.

They drove like that for several minutes, the engine a low murmur beneath the vast quiet.

Then Cork heard it.

Not loud. Not close.

A hum.

It was steady and unfamiliar. Cork straightened. "Dad?"

Dad's shoulders stiffened. He eased off the gas, letting the truck coast.

The hum grew louder.

Ahead, a low rise blocked their view. Dad guided the truck off the road just enough for the grass to swallow its shape. He cut the engine.

Silence rushed in.

The hum crested the rise.

Lights appeared—soft at first, then brighter—sweeping the land in slow, deliberate arcs. Shapes emerged against the darkening sky.

They weren't in a line.

They were circling.

The vehicle rolled over the rise, low and wide, armored and angular—built less like a truck than a weapon. Thick panels overlapped its sides. Heavy tires crushed the grass without slowing. A mounted searchlight swivelled above it, cutting pale white paths across the plains.

And etched into the dark metal at the front—

The symbol.

A circle.

Interlocking arms formed the outer ring, each gripping the next in an unbroken chain. At the bottom, a flame burned in sharp relief. Filling the rest of the circle was a coiled figure, scaled and serpent-like, crowned with a draconic head that seemed to watch even without eyes.

The Circle of One.

Cork's breath caught. He had seen it before—inked into skin, revealed in fear and firelight. Seeing it stamped into steel and moving through the night made his stomach twist.

Without knowing why, he pressed a hand to his pocket, where the disc rested hidden against his leg.

The armored vehicle slowed. The searchlight paused, sweeping across the grass only yards away.

Dad leaned in, his voice barely more than breath. “Don’t move.”

The light passed over them.

Then moved on.

The vehicle rolled forward, its engine humming low as it continued down the road.

Cork’s lungs burned as he finally breathed.

Dad waited several seconds longer than felt possible before reaching for the ignition.

“That was close,” Cork whispered.

Dad nodded once. “Too close.”

The truck rumbled to life. They pulled carefully from the grass, angling away from the road.

They hadn’t gone far when a new sound tore through the air—sharp and cutting, faster than before.

Engines.

Smaller. Faster.

Motorcycles burst from the dark—lean shapes racing across the plains. Two. Then three. Riders crouched low, armored and masked, the same circular emblem marked across their chests and helmets.

“They saw us,” Dad said.

The bikes split wide, fanning out to cut them off.

Dad slammed the accelerator. “Hold on!”

The truck lurched forward, bouncing violently over uneven ground. Headlights flared behind them. Engines screamed.

A beam snapped on, locking onto the truck.

Dad swerved hard.

The truck fishtailed. Tires screamed. Something struck the underside with a sharp metallic clang. Cork was thrown sideways, his shoulder slamming into the door.

The engine sputtered.

“Come on,” Dad muttered.

They plunged into a shallow ravine, dropping hard before slamming up the far side.

There was a sound like the world tearing apart.

Metal screamed. Glass shattered. Cork felt himself lifted from the seat—

Then everything went dark.

***

Cork woke to silence.

Not the tense silence of hiding, but a thick, ringing quiet that pressed against his ears. Pain bloomed behind his eyes as he tried to move. Something warm trickled down his forehead.

“Dad?” he croaked.

The word felt wrong.

He forced his eyes open. The truck lay tilted at an angle, one side crushed into tall grass, the windshield spiderwebbed with cracks. Night had fully settled, stars sharp and distant overhead.

“Dad!”

His father groaned.

Dad was slumped against the door, his face pale, teeth clenched. His left arm hung at an angle that made Cork’s stomach turn.

“I’m here,” Dad breathed. “Just—give me a second.”

Cork scrambled across the cab, pain flaring through his ribs. “Your arm—”

Dad shook his head sharply, then winced. “Don’t touch it.”

They sat there, breathing.

Listening.

No engines.
No lights.
No voices.

The Circle of One was gone.

“They didn’t—” Cork started.

“They thought we were done,” Dad said quietly.

Dad reached with his good hand and turned the key.

Nothing.

He tried again.

The engine didn't even cough.

Dad let his head rest back against the seat. He closed his eyes for a moment. "She's dead," he said. "The truck's done."

Cork looked out through the cracked glass at the dark plains—open, silent, unforgiving.

They had escaped.

But not without cost.

As Cork pressed a shaking hand against his pocket, feeling the hidden disc still there, one truth settled in—

The Circle of One would not stop hunting them.

Even if the road had ended.

Chapter 13
After the Wreck

The wind cut across the plains, cold and relentless, slipping through the broken seams of the truck.

Cork lay still, afraid to move. Every part of him hurt, but the pain felt distant now—dulled, like it belonged to someone else. The silence had changed. It wasn't ringing anymore.

It was listening.

Dad shifted beside him.

Cork turned his head. His father was awake, eyes open, breathing shallow and controlled. His left arm was pulled tight against his chest, his face pale in the thin starlight.

"Dad?" Cork whispered.

"I'm here," Dad said. His voice sounded thick, like it had to force its way out. "Let's—let's stay still for a minute. Just a minute."

Cork nodded, even though Dad couldn't see him.

After a few slow breaths, Dad moved again. "Okay. Help me."

Cork climbed out through the broken side window, the cold biting through his hoodie the moment his feet hit the ground. He turned back and helped Dad out carefully, bracing him when his knees wobbled.

They stood beside the truck for a moment, both breathing hard.

Cork's eyes flicked to the cab. "The map," he said suddenly. "Deborah's map."

Dad lifted his head. "You're right."

He winced and adjusted his injured arm with care. "It's out," he muttered. "Shoulder's dislocated."

Cork swallowed. "Can you fix it?"

Dad shook his head. "Not here."

Cork hurried back to the cab, ignoring the sharp pull in his side as he climbed inside. He grabbed the folded map from the console and shoved it deep into his pocket before dropping back down.

Then he moved to the metal toolbox bolted near the cab. He pried it open and dug through until he found a bundle of old rags—oil-stained, frayed, but strong.

He knelt beside Dad and began tying them together. His fingers were clumsy at first, shaking, but steadied as he worked. Dad watched quietly as Cork looped the sling into place, careful not to jostle the arm.

When it was done, Dad leaned back against the truck, eyes closed.

"I'm sorry," he said quietly.

"For what?" Cork asked.

"For needing you to be strong," Dad replied.

The words settled heavy between them.

Cork looked out across the dark plains. The truck sat crooked and silent—too visible, too exposed. The night felt wide and unfinished.

"Mom used to pray," Cork said suddenly.

Dad opened his eyes.

"She'd say the Creator already knew what was coming," Cork went on, his voice unsteady. "That we just needed help seeing what to do next."

Dad was quiet for a long moment.

Then he nodded. "She did."

They stood there in the wind, heads bowed. Cork didn't know how to pray—not really. So he just spoke. About being scared. About being tired. About wanting to live.

Dad's voice broke when he spoke.

When they finished, the night felt no warmer—but Cork felt steadier somehow.

"We can't stay here," Dad said. "By daylight, they'll come back."

Cork scanned the horizon. In the distance, barely visible, stood the outline of a barn.

“There,” Cork said. “We could hide there.”

Dad followed his gaze and nodded. “Good eye.”

They moved low through the grass, every step measured. The barn grew larger—old and weathered, doors hanging crooked on rusted hinges.

Inside, it smelled of hay and dust and animals long gone. They climbed into the loft and collapsed among the bales, exhaustion pulling them under.

Cork dreamed of his mother.

Not dying—but standing in light, calm and steady.

He woke to barking.

A dog.

Sunlight spilled through the cracks in the boards.

They climbed down and approached the farmhouse cautiously.

The door flew open before Dad could knock.

The farmer stood there with a shotgun leveled at Dad’s chest, his hands shaking just enough to show fear. A dog barked wildly at his feet.

“Don’t come any closer,” the man snapped. “I’ve seen what happens to people who get mixed up in all this.”

“We just need water,” Dad said evenly. “My shoulder—”

“I don’t care,” the farmer cut in. “You’re trespassing. I’m calling the authorities.”

He backed into the house without lowering the gun and slammed the door.

Dad met Cork's eyes.

"Now," Dad whispered.

They ran.

They didn't stop until the farmhouse disappeared behind a rise. Cork's lungs burned. Dad stumbled once, then forced himself onward, teeth clenched against the pain.

***

At the wrecked truck, radios crackled to life.

"Patrol Three, be advised," a voice said. "Report of suspected resistance activity. Trespassers at a farm approximately two miles east of your location."

A pause.

"Understood," came the reply. "Moving to investigate."

***

Cork kept them moving.

They dropped into a shallow drainage ditch, tall grass and shadow swallowing them. Cork stayed low, letting the land guide them away from the farmhouse.

The ditch deepened. Soil gave way to rock. The air cooled.

Ahead, the land opened.

Broken fencing leaned at odd angles, half-swallowed by weeds. Beyond it yawned a wide, stepped hollow—an abandoned quarry, its terraced walls sinking into shadow.

"There," Cork whispered. "Down there."

Dad nodded. "That'll hide us."

They slid down the edge, gravel skittering softly. The stone swallowed sound as they descended, the wind thinning to a breath.

At the base stood several low cement structures—windowless, cracked, doors rusted open like broken mouths.

They slipped inside the nearest one.

Footsteps sounded above them.

Boots in grass. Voices murmuring—close enough to hear, not close enough to understand.

Then engines.

Motorbikes whined along the quarry's rim, the sound bending and echoing off stone.

Dad's hand closed around Cork's wrist.

They sank lower, breathing shallow. Cork bowed his head, heart pounding.

"Creator," he whispered. "Please."

The footsteps passed. The engines circled—once, twice—then drifted away.

They stayed still.

They had learned that much already.

Only when silence returned did Dad finally exhale.

Cold crept back in once the fear faded.

Pale moonlight slipped through a crack in the concrete, thin but steady. Cork gathered debris—boards, rusted tools, a torn tarp stiff with dust—and dragged it closer.

He spread it over them, tucking the edges in.

It wasn't much.

But it cut the wind.

Cork pressed close. Dad shifted carefully, wrapping his good arm around him.

They huddled together on the cold concrete, sharing warmth, the steady rise and fall of Dad's breathing anchoring Cork in the dark.

For the first time since the wreck, the land itself hid them.

And for the moment—

They were safe.

Chapter 14
Shared Light

Morning came slowly.

Sunlight found them before warmth did.

A pale band of gold slipped over the rim of the quarry and spilled across the concrete floor, catching dust in the air and softening it. The cold lingered—the night had sunk too deep into their bones—but the light brought something else.

A sense of having survived.

Cork woke curled beneath the torn tarp, his body stiff and aching, yet calmer than he expected. For a moment, he didn't remember where he was. Only that the world felt still, held together by light.

Then he heard his father's breathing.

Dad sat propped against the wall, eyes open, face pale. His left arm remained bound in the sling Cork had tied the night before. When he noticed Cork stirring, he managed a tired half-smile.

“Hey,” Dad said quietly. “You okay?”

Cork nodded, though his head throbbed when he did. “I think so.” He glanced at Dad’s arm. “You?”

Dad exhaled through his nose. “I’ve been better.”

They sat in silence, listening to the wind whisper through the quarry. Somewhere far off, a bird cried—sharp, lonely.

Cork reached into his pocket for the folded map.

His fingers touched something hard.

Cold.

The disc.

And the paper.

His chest tightened.

He hadn’t planned to say anything—not yet. He’d carried the disc for days, hidden close, as if secrecy itself was protection. But after the night they’d survived—after watching his father bleed and still stand—the weight of it felt heavier than the metal.

Cork looked up.

Dad was already watching him.

“What is it?” Dad asked.

Cork swallowed. His throat felt thick. “There’s... something I haven’t told you.”

Dad didn’t rush him. “Okay,” he said gently. “Go on.”

Cork pulled the disc from his pocket.

Morning light caught its surface—dull gold, worn but unmistakable. The Alpha and Omega were etched deep into the metal, framed by the triangle, the edges notched like a gear. Beneath it, the ancient markings.

Dad stared.

For a long moment, he didn't speak.

"Where did you get that?" he finally asked.

"It was in my room," Cork said. "Under the picture frame. I think… I think Mom put it there."

Dad's breath caught.

Cork unfolded the paper next and handed it over.

Dad read it once.
Then again.

The Kingdom is like a treasure hidden in a field…

His hands trembled.

"She used to write things like this," Dad said quietly. "Not notes exactly. Words she carried with her—old ones. Like they mattered more than anything else."
"You knew?" Cork asked.

"I knew she believed," Dad said. "I didn't understand how deeply."

He stared at the disc, searching its surface as if memory itself might be carved there.

"She started changing about a year ago," Dad said. "Not

in ways people would notice. But she wasn't afraid anymore. She talked about truth like it was solid. Like something no one could take."

Cork's voice dropped. "Is that why they killed her?"

Dad closed his eyes.

When he spoke again, the words came slower. "They questioned her. Asked who she served. What she believed." His voice cracked. "I thought they were trying to scare her."

He swallowed. "She wouldn't deny Him."

Cork's fingers tightened around the disc.

Dad opened his eyes and looked at him fully. "You were right to hide this," he said. "If they find it—"

"I know," Cork said quickly. "But I couldn't keep it from you anymore."

Dad nodded once. "I'm glad you didn't."

"I don't know what it opens," Dad said. "But I know what it is."

Cork frowned. "What?"

Dad tapped the paper. "A witness," he said quietly. "A reminder that your mom chose the King over safety—and that she meant for you to remember what she was willing to lose."

Cork's throat tightened. The disc suddenly felt warmer in his hand, as if it had been waiting for someone to say that aloud.

Dad's eyes flicked to the triangle, the notched edge, the

worn markings. “It isn’t just a trinket,” he said. “And it isn’t just a clue. It’s an invitation.”

The wind stirred, lifting dust across the quarry floor.

Dad shifted carefully, wincing as pain shot through his shoulder. “Whatever this is,” he said, “we don’t chase it blindly. We get to the refuge first. We find people who understand these things.”

Cork nodded.

He slid the disc and paper back into his pocket.

This time, they felt lighter.

Not because they mattered less—

But because he wasn’t carrying them alone anymore.

Chapter 15
By What is Marked

The quarry held them for one more hour.

Not because it was comfortable, but because Dad insisted on listening first.

They sat in the dim cement room while the sun climbed higher, turning the terraced stone outside from gray to gold. Cork kept expecting to hear engines—motorbikes returning, boots on rock, a voice calling down into the hollow.

But the world stayed quiet.

Cork shifted closer to the opening, peering out at the light. "Should we go?" he whispered.

Dad adjusted his position carefully, jaw tight with pain, and raised a hand. "Not yet," he said. "We decide first."

He eased himself down onto a flat slab of stone, wincing as he settled. From inside his jacket, he pulled the folded paper Deborah had given them—the hand-drawn map, creased and smudged, more memory than measurement.

“The map,” Dad said quietly.

Cork crouched beside him, keeping one eye on the quarry rim as Dad opened it.

Deborah’s handwriting ran along the edges in sharp little notes—arrows, warnings, names Cork didn’t recognize. The lines weren’t straight. The distances weren’t exact. It wasn’t meant to be. This wasn’t a map for finding where you were. It was a map for remembering where not to go.

Dad traced one of the bold circles with his finger. “Highway,” he murmured. “Known blockades. Patrol routes.” His finger lingered, then moved away. “We shouldn’t have come this close.”

He followed the pencil line south, then curved east, pausing over blank space. “We ran,” he said. “Hard to tell how far.”

Cork nodded, picturing it.

Dad tapped a small square beside a thin road. “Gas station,” he said. “Watched. That must be how they found us.” He shifted again, then stopped. “We passed near an exit here.”

“So how do we get back?” Cork asked.

Dad followed a broken line that snaked through empty space, then paused. “Deborah said to stay with what she marked,” he said. “Fence lines. Back roads. Landmarks that don’t move.”

His finger hovered over a small notch in the line—no label, just a bend. "This fence runs east near an old windmill," he said. "If we find that, we'll know where we are again."

His finger moved farther along the page, stopping near the corner.

"There," he said.

Deborah had sketched a simple symbol—small, almost careless at first glance.

A triangle.

Not the Circle of One.

A different shape. Familiar in a quieter way.

Cork's hand went to his pocket without thinking.

Dad noticed. "Same shape?"

Cork nodded and eased the disc out just enough for the light to catch it. The triangle etched into the gold gleamed softly.

Dad looked from the disc to the map. "Then maybe that's how we know," he said. "When we're close."

They folded the map again, Dad tucking it back into his jacket.

For a moment, neither of them moved.

Dad glanced toward the quarry rim again, eyes narrowing slightly, listening to the land the way he always did when he was trying to hear what wasn't being said. Cork noticed how he waited now—how he paused before speaking, before moving—as if he knew the smallest mistake could echo farther than it should.

This was different than before.

Dad finally straightened, testing his balance. “All right,” he said quietly, as if speaking too loudly might draw the wrong kind of attention.

Cork nodded, adjusting the strap of his bag.

Whatever lay ahead, it wasn’t just about getting away anymore.

They were walking toward something.

Before moving, Dad nodded toward the far corner of the quarry floor. “Water first.”

They crossed the stone basin carefully until the ground dipped into a shallow hollow. Clear water had collected there, sheltered by the quarry walls. When Cork knelt and dipped his fingers in, the cold bit pleasantly at his skin.

Dad drank slowly, eyes never leaving the rim. Cork followed, cupping water in his hands, letting the coolness steady him as it slid down his throat. For a moment, the tightness in his chest eased.

When they finished, Dad straightened carefully. “All right,” he said. “Now we move.”

They worked east along the quarry wall until the stone dipped low enough to climb. Cork went first, testing each hold, turning back to steady his father when the climb forced Dad to stop and breathe through the pain. When they reached the top, they slipped into a shallow drainage ditch and followed it until the quarry fell behind them.

When Cork finally looked back, it was already hard to see.

Like a bad dream you didn't want to hold onto.

The land opened wide.

Tall grass rolled toward the horizon, broken by fence lines that cut the earth into rough squares. In the distance, wind turbines stood motionless, their blades frozen against the pale sky.

Cork had never seen so much space.

It made him feel small—and watched.

They walked.

After an hour, the land rose just enough to block the horizon. Fence lines disappeared into the grass. The turbines vanished behind low swells.

Cork stopped beside a scraggly cottonwood leaning against a fence. "I can climb," he said. "If I can see the fence line, maybe I can spot the windmill."

He climbed quickly, palms scraped by bark, feet finding holds by instinct. From the higher branches, the world opened again.

Dad's voice drifted up. "See anything?"

Cork shaded his eyes. "There," he said. "Fence first—then the windmill. Maybe a mile."

Dad exhaled. "That's our landmark."

Cork slid back down, steadier now.

They walked again, the fence line guiding them like a quiet promise. The windmill stayed just ahead, growing larger without ever rushing toward them.

Up close, it was older than Cork expected—rusted ribs, bent blades, bolts crusted with age. It creaked softly as the wind shifted.

Dad stopped. "We don't rush in."

They waited.

When nothing followed, Dad rested his good hand against the metal frame. "All right."

Inside the tower's shadow, the air felt cooler. Cork's stomach grumbled.

"We haven't eaten," he said.

"I know," Dad replied.

They sat there for a moment, letting the quiet work on them.

Dad pulled out the map again. "This is where we get our bearings."

They compared pencil lines to fence posts, low hills to the land behind them. Dad traced southeast this time, slower.

"It's not here," he said. "Farther on. Past the canyon Deborah marked."

Cork leaned closer. "What about these symbols?"

Dad followed his finger. "That one warns about a drop—steep ground. And this marks water. Something that lasts."

They folded the map away and stood.

The land waited.

And so did the path ahead.

Chapter 16

A Place Prepared

The ground changed as they followed the map—grass thinning into stone, the land sloping downward into a narrow break in the earth. The path tightened, forcing them closer together.

"Careful," Cork said.

Dad nodded, one hand braced against the rock wall as his shoulder protested the descent. He paused, breathing through it, then waved Cork on. Cork stayed just ahead of him, offering his arm when the footing turned uneven.

The air cooled as they went lower.

Then Cork heard it.

Water.

A thin ribbon of clear water slipped out from beneath a shelf of rock. Cork knelt without thinking, cupping the spring water in his hands and drinking deeply, his lips aching from the cold. Dad joined him, slower, more cautious, then straightened and scanned the walls and the narrow sky above them.

The light dimmed as the stone closed in.

As they stepped away from the spring, Cork noticed a cluster of scrubby trees pressed tight against the rock wall. Their roots twisted into cracks in the stone, clinging where nothing should have grown. Behind them, shadow pooled where the rock curved inward.

Then Cork saw it.

A cave opening cut into the stone ahead.

Faint—but unmistakable.

A triangle carved into the rock framing the mouth.

Cork stopped.

Dad stepped up beside him and stared.

On one side of the entrance, etched deep into the stone, was a single symbol.

An Alpha.

On the other—

An Omega.

Just like the disc.

For a long moment, neither of them spoke.

Dad finally whispered, "We found it."

Cork's hand closed instinctively around the disc in his pocket.

They didn't move.

The cave did not feel empty. Not in the way abandoned places felt—hollow and forgotten. This place felt held. The air was still, carrying the faint sound of water behind them and the distant whisper of wind far above.

Cork hadn't realized how fast his heart had been beating until it began to slow.

He shifted his weight and felt the disc press warm and solid against his leg—heavier than it should have been. Not pulling him forward. Not calling him in.

Just present.

Dad swallowed, his voice barely more than breath. "This wasn't meant to be found by accident."

Cork nodded, though he couldn't have explained why. The thought settled in him without argument. Like stepping onto ground someone else had already chosen for you.

They didn't cross the threshold.

They didn't speak again.

They stood at the mouth of the cave, listening—to the water, to the stone, to the quiet that felt older than either of them.

Knowing, without needing to say it, that this place had been prepared.

And that somehow, they had been brought here.

They had reached the refuge.

Chapter 17
The Refuge

They approached the entrance slowly.

Up close, the cave mouth revealed itself as something more deliberate than Cork had first realized. Stone had been shaped here—not polished smooth, but worked with care. The opening was wide enough for several people to pass through, yet narrow enough to vanish into shadow unless you knew where to look. The triangle etched above it was weathered by time, but not erased.

Dad stopped a few steps short of the threshold.

Cork followed his lead.

For a moment, nothing happened.

Then a voice spoke from the shadows.

"Are you hurt?"

It wasn't loud or sharp. It was steady, like a question

that had been asked many times before.

A figure stepped into the light filtering down from the canyon above. The man wore earth-toned clothing—a short tunic layered with a leather wrap across his chest. It was practical, worn thin at the edges. Not ceremonial. Not threatening.

Two more figures emerged behind him, moving with quiet purpose. Their clothing matched in style, though the colors varied—muted browns, soft grays, deep greens. Not uniforms, but intentional.

Each carried a short sword at their side.

Cork's eyes caught on the blades.

They were double-edged and straight, translucent like glass yet stronger. A faint blue glow ran along each blade—not bright enough to light the cave, but steady enough to be seen. Less a warning than a presence.

Dad shifted, pain tightening his jaw. "My shoulder," he said. "It's out."

The man nodded once. "And the boy?"

"I'm okay," Cork said quickly.

The man's eyes moved between them. "Did anyone follow you?"

Dad shook his head. "We waited. We watched. We came on foot."

The man's gaze dropped—to Cork's pocket.

Cork felt it immediately. The familiar warmth pressed against his leg. Without thinking, he eased the disc out just enough for the light to catch it.

The triangle etched into the gold gleamed softly.

The man inhaled slowly.

"So," he said, quiet but certain, "you found the mark."

He didn't reach for it.

He didn't ask to see it.

He simply stepped aside.

"Come," he said. "You shouldn't stand any longer."

The others moved with him, creating a clear path into the refuge.

Inside, the air changed.

It was warmer, carrying the scent of stone, clean water, and something faintly herbal. The space opened into a broad chamber lit by lanterns set into the walls, each casting a gentle blue-white glow that echoed the light of the guards' blades.

People moved through the chamber quietly. Some wore the same earth-toned clothing as the guards. Others were wrapped in blankets or simple cloaks. Cork saw children near a low fire, an older woman pressing cloth to a man's bleeding arm, hands passing bowls without words.

No one stared.

No one rushed.

Yet everyone noticed.

"Get him seated," the first guard said, already turning

toward a side passage. "We'll set the shoulder."

Dad didn't argue.

Cork stayed close as they guided his father to a stone bench. A woman knelt beside Dad, her movements practiced, her voice calm. "This will hurt," she said gently. "But it needs to be done now."

Dad nodded once.

Cork turned away as she worked, gripping the edge of the bench until his knuckles whitened. Dad's breath hitched, then broke into a sharp cry that echoed briefly through the chamber.

Then it was over.

Dad sagged forward, sweat on his brow, but the pain in his eyes had changed—focused now. Contained.

"Good," the woman said, already wrapping his arm in clean cloth. "It'll heal."

Another set of hands guided Cork toward a basin of warm water. A cloth was pressed into his palms. "Wash," a voice said kindly. "You're safe here."

Safe.

The word felt unfamiliar.

Afterward, they were given clean clothes—simple, soft, warm. Cork hadn't realized how cold he'd been until the fabric touched his skin.

They were led to a long stone table set low to the ground. Bowls of thick stew were passed down the line, followed by bread still warm and water that tasted faintly sweet.

Cork ate slowly at first, afraid the food might disappear if he rushed.

It didn't.

Dad sat beside him, quieter now, his good hand wrapped around the bowl as if anchoring himself.

For the first time since the world had broken, Cork felt something loosen inside him—not relief, not joy, but rest.

He glanced down at the disc resting briefly in his lap, the triangle catching lantern light. He slid it back into his pocket.

This place didn't explain it.

It didn't demand it.

It simply received them.

And for now, that was enough.

Only then did Cork notice what *hadn't* happened.

No one had asked their names. No one had asked what side they were on. No one had demanded an explanation for the disc, the map, or the road that had nearly killed them.

They had been received first.

An older man approached the table. His hair was streaked with gray, his face lined not just with age, but with listening. He carried no weapon. A simple cord hung at his waist, the triangular symbol stitched subtly into the fabric.

"Eat," he said quietly, resting his hand on the table between Cork and Dad. "Questions can wait until bodies are steady." His eyes flicked briefly to Dad's shoulder, then back to Cork. "You've carried enough for one day."

Dad swallowed. "Thank you."

The man inclined his head. "You found us," he replied. "That tells me the Creator is still guiding—even those who have not yet pledged themselves to Him."

Something in Cork's chest tightened—not fear, but recognition.

The man moved on, checking wounds, offering words, never lingering. Cork watched until he disappeared into a passage carved deeper into the stone.

The refuge breathed around them. Quiet footsteps. A child's laugh, quickly hushed but not silenced. Water moving unseen through channels in the rock.

Dad leaned back carefully. "We stay here tonight," he murmured.

Cork nodded.

They were led deeper into the refuge, away from the main chamber and into narrower passages where the air grew warmer and the lantern light softer. The stone walls here were closer, smoothed by countless hands rather than tools. Cork noticed small markings carved into the rock—simple symbols, names, prayers left behind by those who had passed through.

Their quarters were modest but intentional.

Two narrow pallets rested against the far wall, layered

with thick woven blankets. A stone shelf held a clay pitcher of water and a folded cloth. A lantern glowed faintly near the ceiling, its light steady, like a heartbeat you could trust.

Cork ran his hand along the wall, feeling the cool stone beneath his fingers.

"It feels like someone was expecting us," he whispered.

Dad eased onto one pallet with a quiet groan. "Or prepared for people like us," he said.

Cork settled onto the other, pulling the blanket around his shoulders. Only then did he realize how heavy his body felt, how deep the exhaustion ran.

His fingers brushed the disc in his pocket.

Warm. Present.

For the first time, Cork allowed himself to believe they would wake up.

Not to answers.

Not to safety forever.

But to another step.

The refuge continued its quiet work beyond their chamber—tending wounds, sharing food, watching the entrances.

The journey wasn't over.

But here, for this moment, it slowed.

And that mattered.

Chapter 18
Stand Tall

Cork woke slowly—the way you do after a night of deep rest—confused at first, then surprised by the absence of fear.

For a moment he didn't move. The stone ceiling above him was pale and smooth, catching the soft glow of the lamps set into the walls. Their light wasn't harsh or flickering like the world he'd left behind. It was steady.

Safe.

He had dreamed.

Not the fractured, panicked dreams that had chased him since the night everything broke—but a clear one. A quiet one.

His mother stood in sunlight.

Not the burning glare of the desert or the sharp white of explosions, but a warmth that felt alive. She looked the way she always had when she was calm—eyes kind, shoulders relaxed, her presence unhurried. She wasn't rushing him. She wasn't warning him.

She was smiling.

Stand tall, Cork, she had said.

Her voice hadn't been loud, but it carried weight—the kind that settles into you instead of pressing down.

You don't belong to fear.

The words stayed with him as he pushed himself upright.

The room came back into focus. Small. Carved from stone. Thoughtfully arranged. Two low beds. Folded blankets. A basin set into the wall. Everything had its place. Nothing felt temporary.

Cork slid off the bed and crossed the room. As he moved, his eyes caught on something near the basin.

A mirror.

Not glass—polished metal instead, slightly dulled with age. Practical. Honest. Cork almost looked away. He usually did.

But something held him there.

He stepped closer.

At first, he saw the damage.

The thin cut along his cheek, already scabbing. The faint bruise beneath his eye from the wreck. When he turned his arm, the shallow marks where glass had scraped his skin caught the light.

Reminders.

He looked back at his face.

The boy staring at him didn't look older.

But he looked different.

His eyes were steadier. They didn't dart away from the reflection. They held. There was a quiet there that hadn't been before—something settled. Something earned.

Stand tall.

Cork straightened without thinking. His shoulders rolled back. His spine lengthened. The movement felt unfamiliar at first, like stepping into clothing that hadn't been worn yet.

Then it fit.

He wasn't the same boy who had hidden in a closet, counting heartbeats.

He wasn't the same boy who had been carried down the stairs.

He stepped back from the mirror, breathing evenly.

The refuge had a sound—not silence, but something close to it. A distant drip of water through stone. Soft footsteps passing beyond the walls. A low murmur of voices, not urgent, not afraid.

Life moving carefully.

Cork rested his hands on the edge of the basin, studying the lines on his arms again. He remembered his mother tending scraped knees when he was younger, her fingers gentle but sure.

You clean it so it heals right, she used to say. *If you rush it, it leaves a mark.*

He wondered what marks these days would leave.

When he straightened, he noticed the room more fully—the way the stone walls curved instead of meeting in sharp corners, the faint etchings worked into the rock near the doorway. Simple shapes. Lines and angles that felt intentional, though he didn't know why. Whoever had carved this place hadn't done it in a hurry.

Cork crossed to the small opening cut into the wall that served as a window. It didn't look out on the world so much as into the refuge itself—a narrow corridor lit by steady lamps, the stone worn smooth by countless hands. A woman moved quietly through the passage, folded cloth in her arms. She glanced up, met Cork's eyes briefly, and nodded before continuing on.

Something loosened in his chest.

This place wasn't hiding.

It was waiting.

Cork returned to the bed and sat on the edge, careful not to wake his father too abruptly. He watched Dad sleep—the tension eased from his face, his breathing deep and even despite the pain he carried. Cork had never seen him look so tired.

Or so still.

For the first time since the night everything broke, Cork let himself believe that rest might last longer than a few stolen hours.

He didn't know what answers waited beyond this door.

But he knew he was ready to hear them.

Fabric rustled behind him.

Dad stirred, blinking awake, wincing slightly as his injured shoulder protested.

"You up already?" Dad asked quietly.

Cork nodded. "Yeah." He hesitated. "I... I slept good."

Dad gave a small, tired smile. "Me too. First time in a while."

They sat together in the quiet, neither of them needing to fill it.

Then came a soft knock at the door.

Not loud. Not demanding.

Just present.

Dad glanced at Cork, then called, "Yes?"

The door opened partway. A man stood there in earth-toned clothing, his hair streaked with gray, his eyes steady and kind.

"The Overseer is ready to see you," he said gently. "When you are."

Dad drew a slow breath and nodded.

Cork felt his mother's words settle again in his chest.

Stand tall.

Together, they stepped toward the door.

Chapter 19

Before the Answers

They changed quietly.

The clothing the refuge had prepared waited folded on a low stone bench—earth-toned tunics, sturdy trousers, soft boots that felt broken in without being worn out. Nothing ornamental. Nothing that tried to declare who you were. They felt made for walking.

Dad moved carefully as he dressed, jaw tightening when his injured shoulder protested. Cork didn't comment, but he stayed close, ready. When they were finished, Dad rolled his shoulders once and let out a slow breath.

“Ready?” he asked.

Cork nodded.

A guide met them outside their quarters and led them through a series of gently curving corridors. The refuge revealed itself in stages—passages widening, ceilings rising, lamps set deeper into the stone. People moved through the space with quiet purpose. Some nodded as they passed. Others simply observed. No one stared.

They passed the infirmary first.

The air there smelled of clean water and crushed herbs. Men and women worked with practiced calm—washing wounds, binding arms, murmuring reassurance. Cork glimpsed a boy not much older than himself sitting on a stone bench, his leg wrapped carefully, his face pale but steady.

Farther on, the air softened.

The corridor opened into a broad chamber where green life pushed up from the earth. An underground garden stretched beneath a ceiling carved with narrow shafts of light. Real sunlight filtered down in pale columns, warming leaves and soil alike. Water moved through shallow channels cut into the stone floor, feeding rows of greens and small fruiting plants.

Cork slowed without meaning to.

Men and women knelt in the soil, hands dark with earth. Some worked in silence. Others spoke quietly, voices unhurried. Nothing here felt rushed. Nothing felt hidden.

They moved on.

As they passed another branching corridor, Cork heard voices—measured, deliberate. The space beyond opened into what could only be a classroom. Children and adults sat together on low stone benches. At the front, a woman stood beside a wide slab of slate mounted into the wall, chalk marks faint but intentional across its surface.

Symbols. Words. Lines drawn, erased, and drawn again.

Her voice carried.

"...the Creator calls..."

A pause.

"...and the Righteous King..."

Cork's steps faltered for half a breath before he caught himself and continued. The words followed him anyway, settling somewhere unfamiliar and steady.

They entered the heart of the refuge.

The chamber was circular, its walls carved smooth and rising high above them. At the center stood a round table of dark wood, worn soft at the edges by years of use. Light filtered down from an opening far above, dust turning slowly in its beam before settling on the table like an invitation.

An older man waited there.

He rose as they entered.

His hair was silver at the temples, his beard neatly kept. Half-moon spectacles rested low on his nose. His eyes—keen, calm—studied them without urgency. Nothing about him demanded attention, yet the room seemed to steady when he stood.

"I am the Overseer," he said warmly. "You are welcome here."

Dad inclined his head. "Thank you."

"Please," the Overseer said, gesturing to the table. "Sit."

They did.

"Tell me your names."

"Clint," Dad said. "Clint Kingson."

The Overseer nodded. "Clint."

He turned to Cork.

"Cork," Cork said.

One gray eyebrow lifted—not in suspicion, but curiosity.

"Cork?"

"It's a nickname," Cork said quickly. "Just my initials."

The Overseer waited.

"My real name is Cornelius Orion Riley Kingson," Cork added. "Everyone just calls me Cork."

The Overseer smiled, genuine amusement softening his face. "Yes," he said. "That makes sense."

Then, quieter, "Most important names are given before we understand them."

He turned back to Dad. "Tell me about your journey."

Dad spoke carefully at first, then more freely as the Overseer listened without interruption. He spoke of the city, the flight, the roadblocks, the patrols. He did not say everything—but he did not hide the fear.

When he finished, the Overseer nodded once. "You have come far," he said. "Farther than you realize."

He did not speak again right away.

The silence stretched—not heavy, not awkward. Intentional.

The lamps hummed softly. Dust drifted through the shaft of light above the table. Voices echoed faintly from elsewhere in the refuge—teaching, tending, life continuing.

Then the Overseer leaned forward.

He did not look at Dad.

He looked at Cork.

“And you,” he said gently, “do you have any questions for me?”

Cork didn’t answer right away.

Not because he didn’t have questions—but because he suddenly understood that *how* he asked mattered.

The Overseer did not shift. He didn’t glance toward the door or lean back in his chair. He waited—not withholding, not pressing. Present.

Cork felt the disc against his leg, its weight steady and unmistakable. He realized then that the Overseer wasn’t guarding information.

He was guarding *Cork*.

Not from truth—but from receiving it too soon, too raw, before he knew how to hold it.

Cork thought of his mother—how she used to pause before answering him when he was younger. Not to delay, but to listen. To make sure the question came from readiness, not fear.

The Overseer watched him with that same patience.

"There are answers here," the Overseer said quietly. "But answers given too early often become burdens instead of anchors."

His gaze never left Cork's face.

"You will not offend this place by waiting," he added. "And you will not lose truth by asking when you are ready."

Something settled in Cork's chest.

Not clarity.

Permission.

Across the table, his father shifted, instinct pulling him forward. Clint caught himself and went still, jaw tight, eyes fixed on Cork—not to stop him, not to guide him, but to witness.

That mattered more than Cork expected.

"This place does not take words from those who are not ready to give them," the Overseer said calmly. "And it does not silence those who are."

Fear stirred—but it did not take hold.

You don't belong to fear.

Cork reached into his pocket.

He placed the disc on the table.

Then the folded paper beside it.

The gold caught the light. The triangle gleamed—quiet, unmistakable.

No one reached for it.

The Overseer's eyes rested on the disc, then lifted to Cork's face.

"We want to know about these," Cork said.

Chapter 20
What Has Been carried

The room went quiet.

Not the heavy, uneasy silence Cork had come to expect in the days since the world had broken, but a different kind—measured, watchful, almost deliberate. It felt shaped, as if the room itself were holding its breath.

The chamber was larger than Cork had realized when they first entered. The ceiling arched high above them, carved stone smoothed by time and hands. Soft light spilled down from narrow openings far overhead—skylights cut through layers of rock—casting pale beams that drifted like dust through the air. The light did not burn his eyes. It rested.

Cork ran his hand over the wood grain of the table. There were no sharp edges. No ornamentation. Only purpose.

He wondered how many hands had rested there before his. How many stories had been told in low voices, how many hard decisions weighed and left behind in that wood. The table did not feel important because of what it was made of, but because of what it had held.

For the first time since the night the world broke, Cork felt like he was standing somewhere that remembered things longer than fear remembered him.

His hands trembled slightly as he pushed the disc and the folded paper onto the table between them. The metal made no sound when it touched the surface, but Cork felt it anyway—like something settling into place. Like something admitting it had arrived.

The Overseer did not reach for either object.

He leaned back slightly in his chair instead, fingers folded together, his expression unreadable. The half-moon spectacles perched low on his nose caught the light from above, reflecting it back in thin arcs. For a long moment, he simply looked—not only at the objects, but at Cork himself.

Around the room, Cork noticed subtle shifts. One of the guards near the wall straightened. Another lowered his hand from the hilt of his short sword, relaxing rather than tensing. Their tunics were simple, earth-toned cloth, cinched at the waist, practical rather than decorative. Each bore a small stitched symbol over the heart—a triangle, faint but deliberate.

No one spoke. No one moved closer.

Clint noticed it too.

Cork glanced at his father. Dad's jaw had tightened, his eyes flicking briefly to the guards and then back to the

Overseer. Whatever this was, Clint realized, it mattered more than safety. It mattered more than survival.

"You are not the first to carry such things," the Overseer said at last, his voice calm and steady. "But few carry them so unknowingly."

He paused, then added gently, "You are safe here. That does not mean you are finished."

Cork swallowed.

The Overseer's gaze remained on him. "Tell me how you came to have them."

Not *why*.

How.

Cork took a breath and told the story—about the room torn apart, the drawers pulled free, the crushed picture frame. About the folded paper hidden beneath it all, as if waiting. About the disc falling to the floor and the way it had caught the light even then. About the words that made no sense and yet felt like they were meant for him.

As Cork spoke, Clint found himself adding pieces he hadn't planned to share.

"She changed," Clint said quietly. "Not all at once."

The Overseer inclined his head, listening.

"She grew careful," Clint continued. "More thoughtful. She didn't argue. Didn't push. She read at night by the lamp, long after Cork and I were asleep. And when I asked what she was reading..." He swallowed. "She'd smile. Say it was something old. Something true."

Clint's voice roughened. "She never tried to convince me. But I saw it in her eyes. And I saw it again—at the end."

Silence followed. Not awkward. Not empty.

The Overseer nodded once, slowly. "She was known to us," he said carefully. "Not as a name. But her faith is familiar."

Clint's breath caught.

The Overseer reached only for the paper, lifting it with both hands. He unfolded it and read aloud, his voice steady but weighted, each word given its due.

The Kingdom is like a treasure hidden in a field, and when a man has found it, he hides it, returns home, and sells all that he has to purchase the field.

He lowered the paper, letting the words linger.

"These are Ancient Texts," he said. "Older than our walls. Older than the Circle of One. They speak of the Creator."

Cork leaned forward.

"The Creator," the Overseer continued, "is the Beginning. The source of all things. The Alpha. All that exists finds its origin in Him—not merely life, but meaning."

His gaze flicked briefly toward the disc without touching it.

Cork glanced at the etched letter on the metal. He hesitated. "And the other letter?"

The Overseer smiled faintly. “Not yet.”

He folded the paper carefully. “These words are dangerous,” he said, “not because they are false, but because they are true. The Circle of One does not fear rebellion. It fears remembrance.”

He looked directly at Cork. “While I could explain more, truth revealed too quickly often becomes something people try to use instead of something they learn to live by.”

The Overseer’s hand hovered briefly above the disc—never touching—then withdrew.

“This,” he said, “is not a weapon. Not a tool of power. Not even a key in the way most people understand.”

He met Cork’s eyes. “It does not open what is locked away. It reveals what is already present, but unseen.”

Clint frowned. “What is unseen?”

“Truth,” the Overseer said simply. “The truth your wife recognized—and that is now drawing you toward it.”

The Overseer rose slowly from his chair. “I spoke to Cork first because children ask honestly before they learn what answers cost.”

The weight of that settled on Clint—not as a rebuke, but a calling.

“For now,” the Overseer said, “truth can wait. The body cannot.”

He turned toward the doorway, leaving the disc untouched.

"When you are ready to ask the right question," he said over his shoulder, "it will answer."

Cork watched him go, his hand closing around the disc in his pocket.

It hadn't come to the refuge.

He had.

Chapter 21

Between Belief and Belonging

The infirmary smelled like crushed leaves and clean water.

It wasn't the sharp, biting scent Cork remembered from hospitals—no burning sting in his nose, no echoing beeps or hurried voices. Instead, the air felt calm, grounded, as if the stone walls themselves had learned how to breathe.

Cork stayed close to his dad as they were guided inside. The room opened wider than he expected, lantern-light glowing softly along the walls. Low tables lined one side, shelves on the other holding jars of dried herbs, folded cloths, and bowls carved smooth from wood. Everything had a place. Nothing felt rushed.

Clint eased himself onto one of the tables with a quiet hiss of pain.

"Easy," one of the healers said, her voice steady. She wore the same earth-toned tunic as the others, sleeves rolled up, hands already reaching for clean cloth. "Let's see how badly you strained it."

As the sling was carefully removed, Cork looked away at first—then forced himself to watch. His dad's shoulder was swollen and dark with bruising, the skin angry where the impact had twisted it out of place.

The healer pressed gently along the joint, testing movement. Clint's jaw tightened, but he didn't pull back.

"That's enough," she murmured. She reached for a shallow bowl and dipped her fingers into a thick, greenish paste. When she spread it along Clint's shoulder, the smell deepened—earthy, sharp, alive.

Clint let out a breath he hadn't realized he was holding.

"That feels... better," he said quietly, surprise threading his voice.

"It will loosen the swelling," the healer replied. "Rest will do the rest."

Nearby, a basin was set out for Cork.

"Why don't you wash up," someone said kindly. "Those scrapes need cleaning."

Cork rolled up his sleeves and dipped his arms into the warm water. It stung where glass had cut him—but only for a moment. As he wiped away dried blood and dust, he watched it cloud the water, then disappear down a narrow channel carved into the stone.

Clean again.

As he dried his arms, Cork noticed a few children

peeking around the doorway—curious eyes, cautious smiles. One of them whispered something, and another nudged him forward.

“Would you like to meet the others?” a woman asked softly. “They’re just down the corridor.”

Cork hesitated.

He glanced at his dad.

For a heartbeat, fear flared—what if something happened while they were apart? What if safety was temporary?

Clint caught the look and gave a small nod. “Go,” he said. “I’ll be right here.”

As Cork followed the woman down the corridor, Clint watched him longer than he meant to. Only when the bend in the stone swallowed his son from view did Clint let out a slow breath and turn back toward the infirmary.

He settled more fully onto the table, testing his shoulder again. The pain was still there, but muted now—turned down rather than erased.

“How long have you been doing this?” Clint asked the healer quietly.

She glanced up from rinsing her hands. “Here? Or in the world?”

Clint hesitated. “Both.”

She gave a faint, knowing smile. “Long enough to know that bodies heal faster when fear loosens its grip.”

Clint nodded slowly. He looked around the room again—the calm movements, the absence of urgency. "You don't seem surprised when people come in hurt," he said. "Or hunted."

"We grieve," she replied gently. "But we aren't surprised."

"Why?"

"Because darkness resists light," she said simply. "It always has." She paused, then added, "We believe the Creator calls His people to carry light into places the darkness has ravaged—to stand where hope feels thin, and refuse to let it die."

Clint swallowed. "And the Creator," he said carefully. "You speak of Him like He's... near."

The healer met his eyes. "Near enough to be heard," she said. "Not near enough to be forced."

Clint leaned back slightly, letting that settle. "My wife," he said, voice low. "She believed. Long before I ever understood what she was reaching for."

The healer's hands stilled. "Belief leaves marks," she said after a moment. "Not always the kind you can see."

"She died for it," Clint said.

The healer inclined her head—not in pity, but recognition. "Then her faith was already alive."

Clint closed his eyes briefly, then opened them. "My son doesn't belong to any of this yet," he said. "Neither do I."

"No," she agreed softly. "But you are walking the road that leads there."

***

Cork followed the woman down the corridor.

The passage curved gently away from the infirmary and opened into sound.

Laughter.

It hit him so suddenly he nearly stopped walking.

Children were everywhere—running, shouting, crouched in circles, tossing a worn rubber ball in a game Cork didn't know but immediately understood. It reminded him of afternoons before sirens and shadows replaced time.

His chest tightened.

Faces flashed through his mind—friends from school, kids from the neighborhood. A sting burned behind his eyes, sharp and unexpected.

"Hey."

A boy about his age stood in front of him, grinning. "You new?"

Cork nodded.

"I'm Eli," the boy said. "We're playing circle break. You in?"

Cork hesitated—then nodded again.

Soon he was running, dodging, laughing before he realized it. The sound felt strange in his chest, like stretching a muscle he'd forgotten existed. When he finally stumbled to a stop, breathless and smiling, he realized something else too.

He felt lighter.

They sat against the wall afterward, sharing water from a clay cup.

"So where'd you come from?" Eli asked.

Cork shrugged. "A long way."

Eli nodded like that explained everything. "Most people do."

"You live here?" Cork asked.

"Mostly," Eli said. "Some kids come and go. Some stay."

"Why?"

Eli tilted his head. "Because this isn't just a place." He glanced around, lowering his voice. "It's a way of living. People like Deborah go out when it's safe. They bring others back."

Cork's heart skipped. "You know Deborah?"

"Everyone here does," Eli said.

Cork hesitated. "Do you... believe in the Creator?"

Eli shrugged, then nodded slowly. "Yeah. Not always. I listened for a long time first."

"And the King?" Cork asked, stumbling over the words.

Eli smiled. "Him too."

When the meal bell sounded, the children rose together and moved toward the common hall. Cork found his dad waiting there, his arm resting more easily at his side.

They sat among others at long wooden tables. Before

anyone ate, heads bowed—not hurried, not announced.

"Thank you, Creator," someone whispered.

Cork didn't bow his head.

But he listened.

And for the first time in a long while, he wasn't afraid of what he heard.

Chapter 22
The Burning Questions

The questions did not come all at once.

They came slowly, over days, like embers that refused to cool.

The Refuge had a rhythm—quiet mornings warmed by lamplight, shared meals where voices stayed low but steady, hours of work and learning that felt nothing like hiding. It was not the frantic stillness Cork had expected, the kind that waits for disaster to strike. This place breathed. It worked. It listened.

Cork slept better than he had since the world broke. Not deeply at first—his dreams still came in fragments—but enough that the tightness in his chest loosened. Enough that his thoughts no longer raced the moment his eyes closed. When he woke, it was no longer with the certainty that something terrible had happened while he slept.

That alone unsettled him.

Over the first several days, he noticed how people greeted one another—not loudly, not with forced cheer, but with familiarity. Names were spoken carefully, as if they mattered. When meals were shared, someone often murmured thanks to the Creator. Sometimes it was spoken aloud. Sometimes it was only a bowed head and a quiet pause.

Cork never joined in.

No one seemed offended.

As the days passed, he began to notice how often words like *truth* and *light* appeared—not as slogans, not shouted across rooms, but woven into conversation the way weather or time might be mentioned. Ordinary. Assumed. Real.

Eventually, the questions crowded too close to be ignored.

Cork sat across from Eli at a long wooden table carved smooth by years of use. Bread and fruit lay between them, simple and unadorned. Someone nearby whispered thanks to the Creator before eating, and though Cork did not echo the words, he did not feel like an outsider for withholding them.

Eli noticed Cork staring at the table instead of his food.

"You're thinking again," Eli said, tearing a piece of bread.

Cork huffed quietly. "I can't help it."

Eli smiled, not unkindly. "You don't have to."

Cork picked at the edge of the bread with his fingers.

The questions pressed against him, demanding release. "Why does everyone talk about the Creator like they know Him?" he asked at last. "Like He's not just an idea."

Eli didn't answer right away. He chewed slowly, then set the bread down. "Because most of us started where you are now," he said. "Asking whether any of it was more than hope dressed up as certainty."

Cork looked up. "And you?"

Eli nodded. "I chose it."

That word again.

Chose.

"Why?" Cork pressed.

Eli met his eyes. "Because I became convinced it was true."

"That's not the same thing," Cork said. "Believing something is true doesn't make it true."

Eli's smile faded—not in offense, but in recognition. "No," he agreed. "It doesn't."

Silence stretched between them.

"How do you know you're not just telling yourself what you want to hear?" Cork asked. "If the Creator draws people, like everyone says, why doesn't He stop the Circle of One? Why let everything fall apart first?"

Eli exhaled slowly. "Those aren't small questions."

"They don't feel small," Cork said. "They feel heavy. Like if I don't ask them now, they'll crush me later."

Eli studied him for a long moment. “Truth doesn’t break under weight,” he said finally. “Only lies do.”

Cork frowned. “Then why does it feel like everything about truth is... guarded?”

Eli’s fingers stilled.

“Guarded how?”

“Like there are things people won’t say,” Cork continued. “Words they lower their voices for. Knowledge that’s kept back.” He hesitated, then added, “The Ancient Texts. Everyone talks about them, but no one talks about where they come from.”

Eli leaned back slightly.

“They come from somewhere,” Cork pressed. “Words don’t just appear.”

“No,” Eli said. “They don’t.”

He glanced around the room—not out of fear, but habit—and lowered his voice. “The Ancient Texts were preserved from something older. Something whole.”

Cork’s pulse quickened. “What?”

Eli hesitated. Then spoke the words carefully, as though weighing them before release.

“The Book of Light.”

The name landed heavier than Cork expected.

“The Book of Light,” Cork repeated.

Eli nodded. “Not everyone speaks of it openly. Not because it’s forbidden—but because it’s easily misunderstood."

"Is it real?" Cork asked.

"Yes."

"What is it?"

Eli's gaze held steady. "That question is why we don't answer it lightly."

Cork's fingers brushed his pocket, where the disc rested. "Is that where the words come from?"

"They come *through* it," Eli said. "But the Book itself is not the Light."

Cork opened his mouth to ask more, but Eli gently raised a hand.

"There are questions," Eli said, "that grow only when they're carried, not when they're rushed."

Cork leaned back, frustration and curiosity tangling together. "So what am I supposed to do with them?"

Eli stood. "Follow them."

He hesitated, then added, "There's someone you should meet."

Eli didn't slow him down to hide answers—only to make sure Cork would recognize them when they came.

They walked deeper into the Refuge, past corridors older than the others, where the stone felt worn smooth not by tools but by time. The air cooled. The sounds softened. Even Cork's footsteps seemed reluctant to echo.

As they passed, Cork noticed marks etched into the stone—symbols, short phrases, names worn nearly away. People had been here before. Many of them.

They stopped before a simple wooden door, dark with age.

Eli knocked once.

A voice answered from within—strong, steady. "Enter."

The room beyond was small and circular, lit by a shaft of sunlight that fell from a narrow opening high above. Shelves lined the walls, holding scrolls, bound books, and stone tablets etched with symbols Cork recognized —triangles, lines, letters he could not read but somehow felt familiar.

An old man sat near a low stone table, his body bent with age but his presence unyielding. When he looked up, his eyes were sharp—alive with a wisdom that did not rush.

"You've brought a seeker," the old man said.

Eli inclined his head. "I thought it best."

The old man's gaze settled on Cork—not curious, not suspicious. Expectant.

"Sit," he said.

Cork did.

Silence followed—not heavy, not awkward. Waiting.

"You've been hearing words," the old man said at last. "And you want to know what they mean."

Cork nodded. Then, before he could lose his nerve, he

reached into his pocket and placed the disc on the table.

The old man's eyes flicked to it instantly.

He did not touch it.

"Alpha," he said, pointing.

"And Omega?" Cork replied. He hesitated, then added quietly, "I've heard these names before. I just don't know what they are."

"Yes."

"And the triangle?" Cork asked.

The old man's hand stilled. "That," he said gently, "is a question for later."

He looked back at the disc. "The Alpha is the Beginning. The Creator. Before there was order, before there was darkness—He was."

"The Creator spoke," the old man continued, "and Light came into being—not merely illumination, but truth. Meaning. Life."

"But the world was broken," Cork said.

"By choice," the old man replied. "Not by force."

"The Righteous King?" Cork asked softly.

The old man nodded. "He bore the Light—not to compel, but to invite. He came knowing the cost. Not to be crowned, but to be rejected. Not to stand apart from the darkness, but to enter it—to shine the Light as hope for those lost beneath the shadow of evil."

"What happened to Him?" Cork asked.

"He gave Himself," the old man said. "Not what was easy. Not what could be spared. He gave what only He could give—so the way back would remain open."

Cork's voice trembled. "For everyone?"

"Yes," the old man said. "Because without Him, every life remains beneath the shadow of darkness. There is no corner untouched by it, no heart beyond its reach. He came for all—for those who know they are lost, and for those who have yet to realize it."

Cork pulled the folded paper from his pocket and held it out. The old man took it and read the words aloud, his voice steady and unhurried:

"The Kingdom is like a treasure hidden in a field. When a man finds it, he hides it again, and from joy goes and sells all that he has, and buys that field."

When he finished, he folded the paper carefully.

"These words," he said, "come from the Book of Light."

Cork's breath caught.

"But the Book itself is not the Light," the old man continued.

"Then what is it?" Cork asked quietly. "If it isn't the Light itself—what is the Book of Light?"

The old man did not answer at once. He let the question rest between them.

"It is a witness," he said at last. "A record of what the Creator has done, and of the Light the Righteous King carried into the darkness. It does not force belief, and it cannot save by itself—but it reveals the truth to those willing to follow it. It points beyond its pages, and it requires humility to be understood."

Cork hesitated. "If the Alpha is the Beginning," he asked slowly, "then what is the Omega?"

The old man's eyes softened, though his voice remained steady. "Fulfillment," he said. "The promise kept."

Cork frowned slightly, the word settling but not yet clear. "And after that?" he asked. "If there is an end—what happens to those still lost in the darkness?"

The old man regarded him with quiet approval. "There will be time to speak of such things," he said. "More time than you realize."

He paused, then added, "The Creator draws before He explains, and the Righteous King calls before He completes. Let your thoughts rest there."

Cork felt the questions still burning, but something else rose beneath them—something steadier than urgency.

Cork sensed that knowing more right now wouldn't strengthen him—it would only confuse the courage he was still learning how to hold.

The old man rose slowly, leaning on his cane. "Truth is not given all at once," he said. "It is followed."

When Cork stepped back into the corridor, the Refuge felt deeper than before.

Eli glanced at him. "You okay?"

Cork closed his fingers around the disc.

"I think," he said, "I'm more awake than I was before."

Chapter 23
When Darkness is Named

Morning in the Refuge did not announce itself.

It arrived quietly, as it always did—light slipping through narrow stone shafts, the soft echo of footsteps in distant corridors, the low murmur of voices beginning another day of work and watchfulness. Somewhere deeper beneath the Refuge, water moved steadily through unseen channels, a reminder that even hidden places depended on what flowed beyond them.

Cork woke before Dad.

He lay still on the narrow bed, listening. For the first time in days, his body was not drawn tight with fear. The world beyond the stone walls still existed—still hunted, still scarred by fire and loss—but here, for a moment, it felt held at bay.

He turned his head and studied Dad's sleeping face.

Dad looked older than Cork remembered. Not weaker—

just worn. Lines had settled into his face, carved there by grief that had finally found time to surface. Cork thought of his mom then, of the way she used to watch Dad when she thought no one noticed. The same quiet concern. The same unspoken hope that endurance might somehow become enough.

“You’re staring,” Dad said softly, eyes still closed.

Cork startled. “Sorry.”

Dad opened his eyes and looked at him for a long moment. “You sleep okay?”

Cork nodded. “Better than... before.”

Dad sat up slowly, testing his shoulder out of habit. The herbal treatment had helped more than he liked to admit.

“You’re different,” he said at last.

Cork frowned. “Different how?”

“Quieter,” Dad said. “But not scared.” He shook his head slightly. “Your mom used to look like that sometimes. Like she was listening to something the rest of us couldn’t hear.”

He hesitated, then added more quietly, “She asked questions too. The kind that don’t leave you alone once they start.”

Cork swallowed. “I don’t mean to,” he said. “It’s just... they’re there. When I wake up. When I try not to think.”

Dad studied him, something conflicted passing behind his eyes. “I can see that,” he said. “I see you wrestling with things that don’t have easy answers.” He exhaled slowly. "Part of me wants to tell you to be careful. To stop digging before it costs you something."

He looked away for a moment, his jaw tightening. "That road took your mother somewhere I couldn't follow. And I was afraid it would take her from me."

Cork's chest tightened. "Did it?"

Dad shook his head slowly. "No. Not really." He looked back at Cork. "But it changed her. Strengthened her in ways I didn't understand. And I see that same strength starting to take root in you."

He rested his forearm on his knee. "I don't know if I believe what she believed," he admitted. "I'm still not sure I can. But I won't stop you from asking. From searching. I'd rather you walk that road honestly than pretend the questions aren't there."

Cork didn't know what to say.

Dad reached out and squeezed his shoulder. "Just don't walk it alone," he said. "Whatever you find."

A knock sounded at the door—not sharp, not urgent, but firm enough to demand attention.

"The Overseer requests your presence," a calm voice said from beyond the stone. "When you are ready."

***

They walked together through the Refuge, deeper than Cork had gone before.

The corridors twisted and widened, then narrowed again, bending in ways that made it impossible to keep a straight sense of direction. Here, the stone walls bore faint carvings—names, symbols, short prayers etched by hands long since gone. Lanterns hung at uneven intervals, their light steady and warm, casting shadows that shifted as people passed.

The Refuge was awake.

Not frantic. Not afraid. Awake.

Voices drifted through the corridors—low, purposeful, measured. Cork caught fragments as they passed: questions asked and answered, plans weighed, words chosen carefully. This was not a place bracing for disaster. It was a place accustomed to vigilance.

As they passed a narrow side chamber, Cork slowed.

A small group stood gathered around a rough table scattered with chalk-smudged slates. No single voice led the conversation. One traced symbols quickly while others interrupted, questioned, and corrected. Learning, not instruction.

As Cork moved past, a single sentence reached him, spoken quietly but with conviction:

"...the Righteous King brings Light where darkness believes it has already won..."

The words lodged in his chest.

Dad noticed and placed a hand gently on his shoulder. "Later," he said under his breath.

Not as a dismissal—
as a promise.

They did not go straight to the Overseer.

Instead, the guide led them through a series of working corridors, places Cork hadn't yet seen. Narrow storage chambers stacked with sealed jars. Racks of tools cleaned and sorted by size and purpose. A watch post carved into the stone where two sentries stood without speaking, eyes fixed on a narrow slit that looked out toward the land beyond the Refuge.

No one hurried.

No one wasted movement.

Cork noticed how often people touched one another's shoulders in passing—not affectionately, not urgently. Just contact. Presence.

In one chamber, an older man sharpened blades while a younger woman checked them, testing balance and edge before placing each one back into its slot. In another, two boys hauled buckets of water along a stone channel, laughing until an adult gave them a look that wasn't angry, just expectant. They quieted immediately and kept working.

Work mattered here.

Not as punishment.
As stewardship.

Cork found himself handed a coil of rope and gestured toward a rack that needed sorting. He hesitated only a moment before stepping forward. No one explained how. He watched, adjusted, learned. When he finished, the man beside him nodded once and moved on.

That was all.

The nod stayed with him.

As they walked again, Cork realized something else: no one here asked him who he was.

Not his name.
Not his past.
Not what he believed.

They acted as though his presence alone carried responsibility.

That unsettled him — and steadied him at the same time.

At a junction in the corridor, they paused to let a group pass. A woman carried a tray of wrapped cloths stained dark with old blood. Her face was tired but focused. When she noticed Cork watching, she gave him a brief smile.

“Morning,” she said.

“Morning,” he replied, surprised at how natural it sounded.

When they moved on, Dad leaned slightly closer. “You see it,” he murmured.

Cork nodded. “They don’t hide.”

“No,” Dad said. “They prepare.”

Something in Cork loosened then.

Not fear.
Not doubt.

Resistance.

The kind that comes from realizing belief might cost him something real.

And that, somehow, made it feel truer — not less.

They entered the heart of the Refuge.

The chamber was lower and wider than the others, its walls cut straight instead of curved, its ceiling reinforced with thick stone beąms. This space had not grown naturally—it had been shaped. Maps covered much of the room, some carved directly into the rock, others sketched on stretched hides and pinned in place with metal spikes. Symbols, routes, and markings overlapped one another, layered with urgency rather than beauty.

A long rectangular table dominated the center, scarred by years of use and crowded with rolled parchments, tools, and weighted stones.

The Overseer stood at the head of the table, posture alert, hands resting flat against the wood.

Nearby waited a broad-shouldered man in muted earth-toned armor. A short double-edged sword hung at his side, its blade shimmering faintly with a pale blue glow —less decoration than readiness.

"The Captain of the Watch," the Overseer said.

Before anyone could speak further, the calm fractured.

Footsteps echoed sharply from the corridor beyond—fast, uneven, urgent. The scrape of boots against stone. Breath pushed hard through lungs that hadn't slowed.

Several heads turned.

Deborah entered the chamber.

Dust clung to the hem of her cloak. A smear of grime marked her cheek where she had wiped sweat without stopping. She did not pause. She did not sit.

"They're moving," she said.

The room stilled.

"North and east," Deborah continued, already unrolling a narrow strip of hide. "And yes—they're closer than yesterday."

She marked lines with the blunt end of a dagger. "Patrols are doubling along trade routes. Not marching yet—testing."

"Testing?" Dad asked.

"Communities," Deborah replied. "Safety first. Unity. Peace." Her blade traced a circle. "They mix truth with lie until people can't tell which is which."

"They call the Ancient Texts outdated," she added. "Say the Righteous King was only a teacher. Not one with the Creator."

"False refuges," the Captain said.

Deborah nodded. "Places that feel safe until it's too late."

Cork felt his chest tighten.

The Overseer drew a slow breath. "Then we speak plainly."

***

"The Circle of One did not begin with these movements," the Overseer said later. "They are ancient."

Before cities.

Before kingdoms.

Before even the Ancient Texts.

Cork leaned forward.

The Overseer placed a metal disc on the table.

Cold. Dark. Deliberate.

The Seal of the Circle of One.

Cork recognized it instantly—skin, steel, pursuit.

“They call this unity,” the Overseer said. “But it is belonging without righteousness.”

“And the serpent?” Cork asked.

“The deceiver,” Deborah said. “The adversary.”

Dad interrupted, skeptical. “If he offers light, why does everything rot?”

The silence that followed was not reprimand.

It was acknowledgment.

“Because false light reveals nothing,” the Overseer said. “It only blinds.”

Dad absorbed that.

Cork felt something shift inside him—not understanding, not belief—but alignment.

If the enemy offered light, it was because real Light existed.

“Yes,” the Overseer said softly, noticing Cork’s grip on his pocket. “That disc has meaning here.”

He did not explain.

"And so," the Overseer said, meeting his gaze, "your questions matter."

Not because answers were being withheld.

But because timing mattered as much as truth.

Chapter 24
Where Truth Stands

Truth was not rare here. No one acted as though it needed protecting, as though it might vanish if handled too roughly. It was spoken aloud, read from the Ancient Texts, written on scraps of paper and passed from hand to hand. The words were offered freely, again and again.

Children learned the word early. Adults spoke it without ceremony. It was part of the Refuge's language, like *watch* or *harvest* or *rest*.

What Cork had never noticed was the choice hidden inside it—not whether truth would be offered, but whether it would be received.

But not everyone received them.

Some passed through the Refuge and left unchanged. Others stayed for years and never crossed the threshold that mattered most. Truth waited—patient, unoffended —until a heart was willing to stop resisting it.

Cork first felt the weight of that distinction while helping Eli repair a cracked lantern frame.

They worked side by side in comfortable silence, Eli steadying the metal while Cork tightened the fastenings. The task was ordinary, almost forgettable—and somehow that made it feel important.

Eli spoke without looking up. "You've been asking better questions lately."

Cork frowned. "Better how?"

"Slower," Eli said. "You're letting them sit."

Cork considered that. "I don't think truth shows itself to people who rush it."

Eli's mouth curved slightly. "No. It doesn't."

They worked a little longer before Cork spoke again. "Everyone here talks about truth like it's something you follow. Not something you keep."

"Because it is," Eli said simply.

Cork hesitated. "Then what's the Sanctuary?"

Eli set the lantern down and wiped his hands. "It isn't a place where truth is hidden."

Cork waited.

"It's the place where truth finally has nothing left to fight against," Eli continued. "Not walls. Not enemies. Not noise."

He paused, choosing his words. "The Sanctuary offers truth freely. The only thing that can keep someone from receiving it is their choice to turn away."

That wasn't what Cork expected.

"So it's... underground?" he asked.

Eli shook his head. "You're still thinking in directions."

He leaned back against the stone wall. "Truth doesn't need guarding. It stands on its own. What stands in the way is the heart."

Cork thought of the folded paper he carried—the Ancient Text, worn soft from being handled. The words had been there all along. Nothing about them had changed.

"Then why doesn't everyone understand it?" Cork asked.

"Because understanding isn't the same as receiving," Eli said. "Truth confronts before it comforts. Some people would rather turn away than be named by it."

Cork's fingers brushed his pocket, resting briefly against the disc.

The weight of it felt different than before.

Later, while returning the lantern to its hook, Cork found Mara sorting dried herbs along a low table. She worked with steady focus, separating leaves by scent alone.

Cork hesitated beside the table, watching the care with which she handled each leaf, as if none were interchangeable.

"Can someone know the truth," Cork asked quietly, "and still walk away from it?"

Mara didn't look up. "All the time."

He swallowed. “Why?”

“Because truth asks for faith,” she said. “And faith asks for surrender.”

She paused, then added, “Everyone is shown truth. Not everyone is willing to let it change them.”

Cork hesitated. “When you entered the Sanctuary—did you understand everything?”

Mara smiled faintly. “No.”

“What did you understand?”

“That the truth I was looking for wasn't hidden from me,” she said. “It was hidden by me.”

Her hands stilled.

“I had to stop defending myself long enough to listen.”

That night, Cork lay awake longer than usual.

The Refuge was quiet—stone, lamplight, the distant sound of water beneath everything. Dad slept nearby, breathing evenly.

Cork stared at the ceiling, his thoughts circling.

Truth offered.
Faith required.

The disc rested against his palm as his fingers curled unconsciously around it.

Somewhere deep within the Refuge, truth stood unmoving.

And Cork wondered how long it would take him to stand with it.

Chapter 25
The Table of Trust

By the time Cork stopped counting the days, he realized something quietly reassuring.
The Refuge had begun to feel normal.

Not in the way the world used to feel normal—no bright screens, no traffic, no Saturday routines or school bells that meant nothing more than time passing.

Normal in a different way.

A steady rhythm. Work that mattered. Faces that carried fear quietly instead of letting it rule them. Meals shared without hurry, as if even eating had become an act of resistance against the darkness beyond the stone.

Cork still carried the disc in his pocket. He still woke some mornings with his heart racing, the memory of fire and running clinging to him like smoke. But more often now, he woke to lamplight and stone and the sound of water moving far beneath the Refuge, and he remembered where he was.

Safe.

Dad liked the word.

Cork noticed it in the way Dad's shoulders rested lower, in the way he no longer scanned every corridor as if soldiers might spill from the walls. He heard it in the way Dad spoke to people now—still cautious, still guarded, but no longer sharp at the edges.

"You're starting to trust them," Cork said one evening as they carried baskets of folded cloth back toward their quarters.

Dad gave him a sideways look. "I'm starting to appreciate walls that don't burn."

Cork almost smiled.

Almost.

Because beneath the steadiness, the questions were still there. Not shouting anymore. Whispering. Rising when he overheard a phrase in the corridor or caught a quiet thanks to the Creator spoken over a meal. Sometimes they pressed so close he had to stop and breathe.

He kept thinking about the Overseer's words.

Your questions matter more than ever.

It felt strange—being told that questioning wasn't weakness. That it might be necessary.

That morning, Cork volunteered to help with lunch.

Not because he was especially skilled, but because he asked.

The Refuge did not coddle people, even the new ones. It

offered shelter and healing—and then it offered responsibility.

Cork followed Mara down a corridor that smelled faintly of baked grain and herbs. He had seen her often enough now to recognize her steady pace and quiet strength, the kind that came from carrying heavy things and learning when to set them down.

"You've got strong hands," she said without turning.

Cork blinked. "I do?"

Mara nodded once. "You wouldn't have made it here if you didn't."

He didn't know what to do with that, so he adjusted his grip on the basket she handed him.

Inside were smooth wooden bowls, stacked carefully.

They entered the broad hall that served as the Refuge's communal gathering space. It wasn't grand, but it was warm. Lanterns hung from iron hooks. Long wooden tables ran in rows, scarred and polished by years of meals and conversations.

People filtered in gradually. Some laughed softly. Some spoke in low voices. Children wove between benches, carrying cups too carelessly, earning gentle corrections and quiet smiles. Others said nothing at all, but their silence didn't feel empty.

Truth here was not hidden. It was spoken plainly, passed freely—heard by anyone willing to listen.

Cork set bowls and cups, watching hands place bread, fruit, and stew at the center of each table. He noticed how easily people made room for one another.

How no one pushed.

How no one hoarded.

It was strange.

And it tightened his throat.

Dad arrived later, scanning the room out of habit—then relaxing when he saw Cork.

“There you are,” Dad said.

Cork lifted one shoulder. “They put me to work.”

Dad’s mouth curved. Almost a smile. “Good.”

They sat near the middle of the hall.

Cork watched people settle in. He recognized faces now —men and women who nodded as they passed, children who whispered his name like he already belonged. Eli caught his eye from another table and lifted a hand before turning back to a quiet conversation with two younger boys.

Then Cork noticed someone he didn’t recognize.

That alone shouldn’t have mattered. There were still people he hadn’t met.

But Cork realized, after a moment, that he hadn’t seen the man before at all—not yesterday, not in the days since the Refuge had begun to feel familiar.

And yet the man moved as if he already knew the rhythms.

He sat comfortably across the room, folding his hands

on the table as though he had done it many times here. He wore earth-toned clothing like the others. His hair was dark, cut short. His face was ordinary enough that Cork's gaze kept sliding off it.

Not threatening.

Just... unremarkable.

Cork caught fragments of the man's voice drifting across the hall as he wiped the table nearby.

"New faces," the man said easily. "That's a good sign."

Cork kept working, stacking bowls, wiping a spill, moving on. But the words carried.

"You'll find the Refuge is a gift," the man continued. "A place of rest in a world that won't stop taking."

The words were right. The order was right.

But they landed like something memorized rather than lived.

Around the man's table, a few people nodded. Someone murmured agreement.

"I help where I'm needed," the man went on. "A little here, a little there. It's good to belong to something steady."

Cork shifted the basket on his hip. He noticed the man's hands—calm, deliberate—breaking bread with practiced care, as if performing something familiar.

"It's rare," the man said, "to find a community that doesn't demand too much. That doesn't weigh people down with expectations."

Cork wiped the table harder than necessary.

That sentence should have sounded comforting.

And in a way, it did.

But it left something hollow behind it.

“Out there,” the man continued, gesturing vaguely, “everyone’s always searching for something higher. Something beyond themselves.” He chuckled softly. “But here? Here you can finally breathe. Finally be safe. No more chasing. No more needing to prove anything. Truth doesn’t have to be so demanding.”

Cork straightened.

The last sentence lingered longer than the rest.

Not because it was cruel.

But because it asked nothing of him.

He glanced instinctively toward Dad. Dad was listening —not intently, not suspiciously—but with the tired openness of someone who wanted the words to be true.

Across the room, Mara caught Cork’s eye and lifted her chin slightly.

You alright?

Cork nodded.

He told himself he was being unfair. Not everyone spoke the same way. Not everyone chose words carefully.

Still, he realized no one else in the Refuge spoke of truth like that—not as something weighty, but as something inconvenient.

The man's voice blended back into the hum of the hall.

Cork returned to his work, hands moving automatically while his thoughts lagged a step behind, turning the words over as if they might change shape.

He wasn't afraid of the man.

He was afraid of how easily the words could settle without asking anything in return.

Life continued.

And Cork tried to let himself believe in the calm of it—because believing felt easier than choosing.

Chapter 26
The Weight of Truth

The rest of the day unfolded without interruption. If anything, it felt quieter.

Not because the Refuge had grown empty, but because Cork had stopped straining to listen for danger in every sound. Footsteps in the corridor were simply footsteps. A lantern being adjusted on its hook was only a lantern. Even the distant rush of water far beneath the stone felt less like a warning and more like a heartbeat the Refuge had carried for a long time.

Normal.

He should have been grateful for it.

He was.

And still, his mind kept returning to one sentence—calmly spoken across a room as if it were kindness.

Truth doesn't have to be so demanding.

The words followed him through the day like dust that wouldn't shake loose.

Cork spent the afternoon where he was assigned—sorting supplies in a storage room stacked with crates, carrying water to a work hall where hands were busy repairing straps and stitching cloth, returning tools to their places so no one had to search for them later. The work was simple and repetitive, the kind that usually let his thoughts drift.

But his thoughts didn't drift.

They circled.

He kept replaying the man's voice. Not the volume, not the accent—there hadn't been anything remarkable about either. What bothered Cork was how practiced the sentence had sounded, as if it had been spoken before, shaped to fit more than one room.

It offered relief.

And relief had a way of sounding like truth when you were tired.

At some point, Cork found himself touching the disc through the fabric of his pocket. Not taking it out—just feeling its familiar edge, the gear-like ridges pressing against his thumb.

He didn't know why it steadied him.
He only knew that it did.

In a corridor outside the storage rooms, Cork paused beside a narrow shelf where someone had left a folded scrap of paper. The ink was faded, the corners worn soft, as if it had been carried in many pockets before finding a resting place.

He recognized it.

Not the paper itself, but the words.

The same Ancient Text he had once unfolded after finding it tucked inside the broken picture frame in his bedroom.

Cork read it silently, letting his eyes move over the lines the way his fingers had once traced the symbols on the disc.

The Kingdom is like a treasure hidden in a field...

He stopped halfway through, swallowing.

The words had not changed.
And yet they felt heavier today.

He folded the paper carefully and set it back where it had been, as if returning it to someone's hand.

Truth was not scarce here.
It was everywhere.

What wasn't everywhere was the willingness to let it cost.

Later, as the evening meal ended and people began clearing the hall, Cork was assigned to help again. He carried bowls to the wash room, stacked cups, wiped benches, and tried not to look across the room.

He didn't want to search for the man.

And he didn't want to find him.

But when Cork lifted his eyes, he saw the stranger

anyway—already standing, already moving as if he knew when to rise and when to linger, speaking to someone with that same practiced ease.

Cork's stomach tightened.

Not fear.

Not danger.

But something close enough to danger that his body noticed before his mind did—a warning he couldn't explain.

He turned away and focused on his work.

His hands moved.

His thoughts lagged behind.

When the last of the tables were wiped and the hall began to empty, Cork found Mara near the side passage where linens were stacked. She gathered them steadily, folding with the same careful attention she'd given her herbs.

"You're quiet today," Mara said.

Cork gave a small shrug. "I'm not sure what to do with what I heard."

Mara didn't ask who.
She didn't need to.

They walked together, their footsteps soft on the worn stone.

"You hear a lot when you're working tables," she said again, not accusing him—just naming what was true.

Cork hesitated. “Is it that obvious?”

Mara’s mouth curved faintly. “Only to someone who’s been listening their whole life.”

They passed a small group of children sitting cross-legged near a corridor bend, waiting for a lesson to begin. One of them waved at Cork with a grin. Cork lifted his hand in return, surprised by how quickly that had become normal too.

Mara watched him, then said quietly, “You’re starting to belong.”

Cork’s throat tightened. “I don’t know if that’s the same as believing.”

“No,” Mara said. “It isn’t.”

They walked a few more steps before Cork spoke again, unable to keep the question behind his teeth.

“Where did you come from?”

Mara slowed near a stone alcove and set the linens down carefully, as if the answer deserved the same care.

“Not here,” she said. “Not originally.”

Cork waited.

“I came with my family,” she continued. “My husband. Three children.”

Cork nodded slowly. He tried to picture it—three children walking into these corridors for the first time, wide-eyed, frightened, hopeful.

“Two of them, a son and daughter, are still here,” Mara said. “Grown now, though they don’t feel it to me.”

"And the third?" Cork asked quietly.

Mara's gaze drifted somewhere past him, toward a place only she could see.

"My husband was a guard," she said. "Not here at first. We lived at another refuge, smaller than this one. Less stone. More wood. More open sky."

Cork's chest tightened.

"It was attacked," Mara went on, her voice steady even as her fingers clasped tighter around the folded linen. "Not like the world attacks with sudden noise. It began with softness. With words. With promises. People who sounded gentle. People who spoke of unity and belonging."

"They arrived before the soldiers did," Mara said. "And when the soldiers came, many had already surrendered without realizing it."

Cork's stomach turned.

"When the breach happened, my husband held the inner passage," Mara continued. "He kept the sentinels from reaching the families. He bought time."

"For dozens," Cork whispered.

Mara nodded once. "For dozens."

"And he—"

"He didn't survive," she finished simply. "But many others did."

Silence settled between them.

The words from the Sage stirred in Cork's memory.

He gave Himself.

Cork's voice came out rougher than he meant it to. "He sounds like the Righteous King."

Mara looked at him then—really looked at him.

"Yes," she said softly. "In a small way. All true courage reflects Him."

Cork swallowed. "Why would someone give themselves like that?"

Mara's eyes held his. "Because love does not count the cost the way fear does."

Cork swallowed hard. His voice came out barely above a breath. "My mom gave her life too."

Mara didn't hesitate. She stepped forward and wrapped her arms around him, holding him with the steady, familiar strength of a mother who understood grief without needing it explained. Cork stood still at first, then let himself lean into it.

When she finally released him, Cork looked down at his hands.

He thought of the Righteous King entering darkness.

Not to crush it.
To bring light.
To rescue those who could not rescue themselves.

He felt the question rise again—hot and heavy.

"And your other child?" Cork asked, unsure why the question pressed forward.

Mara's hands folded together. "He was shown the

truth," she said.

"The Sanctuary does not hide it," Cork murmured, remembering Eli's words.

Mara nodded. "Truth was offered to him freely."

"But he didn't accept it," Cork said.

"No," she replied.

Cork waited for anger in her voice.

There wasn't any.

"It did not make sense to him," Mara continued. "A Creator who allows evil. A King who saves through surrender. He wanted answers before faith."

Cork's fingers brushed the disc again.

"He said it was not logical," Mara said, and for the first time there was a faint ache beneath the steadiness. "He said if the Creator was real, then the world would not be this broken."

Cork stared at the stone floor.

"And what did you say?" he asked.

Mara exhaled slowly. "I said the world is broken because we chose darkness. And the Creator did not leave us there."

Cork's chest tightened.

"But my son couldn't bear a truth that asked him to bow," Mara finished quietly. "So he found a lie that let him stand tall."

Cork's thoughts flashed to the stranger's words.

No more chasing. No more needing to prove anything.

A lie that let him stand tall.

“There are rumors,” Mara went on, lowering her voice, “that he joined a fortress that drifts above the earth. A place that promises certainty without surrender.”

A thought brushed the edge of Cork’s mind—certainty without surrender.

It sounded disturbingly close to something he had already heard.

Cork didn’t ask more.
Some truths felt heavy enough already.

Mara gathered the linens again and started walking.

“Do you hate him?” Cork asked suddenly.

Mara stopped.

“No,” she said. “I grieve him.”

Then, softer, “And I pray the same truth he rejected will one day be the truth that frees him.”

They walked the rest of the corridor without speaking.

When Cork finally returned to his quarters, the lamps were low and the air was cool. Dad was awake, sitting on the edge of the bed, rubbing his hands together as if warming them.

“You’ve been thinking,” Dad said.

Cork sat beside him. For a moment he didn’t speak. He didn’t know where to begin.

Then he said, “Do you ever worry that believing

something might cost too much?"

Dad was quiet for a long time. In the dim light, Cork could see the tension in his jaw.

"I worry about losing you," Dad said at last. "I worry that if you follow this all the way, it will take you somewhere I can't protect you."

Cork nodded, feeling the weight of it.

"And I worry," Dad added, voice lower now, "that I've seen this road before."

Cork's heart thudded. "Mom."

Dad didn't deny it.

"Your mother used to look at the world like she could see through it," Dad said quietly. "Like the darkness was real, but not final. It made her brave in ways I didn't understand."

Cork swallowed.

"And it cost her," Dad said.

Cork's throat tightened. "But it also—"

"It also gave her something," Dad admitted. "Strength. Peace. Something that didn't disappear when everything else did."

Dad stared at his hands.

"I don't know if I believe what they believe," he said. "But I can see why people would want it to be true."

Cork looked at him. "And you want me to keep asking."

Dad lifted his eyes. "Yes."

"Even if you're afraid?"

Dad let out a short breath that might have been a laugh, if it hadn't carried so much weight. "Especially because I'm afraid."

Cork nodded slowly.

He wanted to tell Dad about Mara's husband.
About her son.
About the way truth could be offered freely and still refused.

But the words tangled inside him.

So he only said, "I heard someone today say truth shouldn't be so demanding."

Dad's brow furrowed. "And?"

Cork's voice dropped. "And part of me wanted to believe him."

Dad didn't answer right away.

When he did, his voice was careful. "That's how lies work, Cork. They don't sound like lies at first."

Cork looked away.

Dad's hand rested briefly on his shoulder.

"I can't tell you what to believe," Dad said. "But I can tell you this—your mother never chose what was easy. She chose what was true."

Cork lay back on his bed, staring into the dim light.

Dad settled onto his own bed and the room grew quiet.

But Cork did not sleep.

Mara's words pressed in from one side—truth offered, faith required, surrender that did not promise safety. Eli's voice joined them, steady and clear.

And from the other side came the stranger's voice, calm and reasonable.

Truth doesn't have to be so demanding.

The sentence returned again and again, softer each time, easier to hold.

Cork turned onto his side. Then onto his back.

His hand brushed against the small stuffed rabbit tucked near the edge of his bed—the fabric worn thin, one ear bent just slightly out of shape. He hadn't thought about it in days, and the familiarity of it tightened something in his chest.

Somewhere deep within him, a question waited—not about what was true.

But about what he would choose.

And Cork tossed and turned until the darkness behind his eyes began to move.

Chapter 27
The Dream

Cork dreamed before he realized he was dreaming.

At first, it felt like remembering.

He was small again.

Not small as in weak, but small as in young—young enough that the world still felt safe simply because his parents were near. He stood in a wide open place beneath a sky washed pale blue, the air warm against his skin. Somewhere nearby, someone laughed. The sound carried easily, unafraid of being overheard.

The rabbit was in his arms.

But not as it was now.

In the dream, it was new.

The fabric was clean and soft, its seams straight and unbroken. Both ears stood tall, unbent, the glass eyes clear and bright. It smelled faintly of something warm and familiar—home, before home had become a memory. He remembered the moment it had been placed into his hands, too big for his grip, his fingers barely able to wrap around its body. He had laughed then, surprised by the weight of it, by how quickly it became his.

The dream did not stay still.

Time folded in on itself, the way it only can in memory.

The rabbit changed.

The fabric thinned where his fingers held it most. One ear bent slightly, never quite standing straight again. A small tear opened along its side.

He saw his mother sitting nearby, the rabbit resting in her hands now instead of his. She worked carefully, needle and thread moving with quiet patience as lamplight pooled around her fingers. He could almost hear the soft scrape of thread through fabric, almost feel the stillness of the moment.

She looked up and smiled at him.

Not the quick kind of smile, but the kind that lingered in her eyes. The kind that said he was safe. That his father was safe. That whatever waited beyond the edges of the world had not reached them yet.

Cork felt that smile settle somewhere deep in his chest.

The dream shifted.

Heat pressed down on him.

He sat in the back seat of the old truck as it rattled eastward, the road stretching endlessly ahead. Sunlight poured through the windows, baking the cracked vinyl seats, the air thick with dust and sweat. His dad's hands were tight on the wheel. His mom reached over once, resting her fingers on his arm.

It was the last time Cork remembered the world feeling ordinary.

The rabbit rested in his lap. He traced its ear absentmindedly, watching the horizon blur.

Then the dream fractured.

The Oasis burst into view—lantern light swinging wildly against stone, shadows tearing across the walls. Shouts collided in the dark. Fear snapped through the room like a breaking wire.

Cork saw himself there—smaller, younger—pressed close to his dad, his fingers locked around the rabbit's ear as if it were the only solid thing left.

He was not inside the memory.

He hovered above it.

Watching.

He saw the man near the entrance. Calm amid chaos. His voice smooth even as hands grabbed at him, even as his jacket was torn away.

A flash of skin.

A mark.

The tattoo.

It curved dark against flesh—circular, closed, deliberate. Simple. Pulling.

Child-Cork did not understand why his stomach

tightened.

Older Cork did.

The memory vanished.

Another took its place.

Running.

Stone beneath his feet. Breath burning his lungs. The rabbit clutched tight as fire leapt where it should not have been. Flames crawled along walls and doorways, not warming, not guiding—devouring.
This fire did not give light.

It consumed it.

Above it all, Cork watched.

He saw how close the danger had always been.

How innocence had survived not because it was strong—but because it had not yet been claimed.

The child-Cork looked up.

For a moment, their eyes met.
The distance between them felt vast.

The rabbit's glass eyes reflected a light not born of flame.

The dream tilted.

And Cork fell into himself.
The table appeared.

Long. Wooden. Familiar.

Lanterns glowed overhead. The murmur of voices filled the hall. Everything was exact—too exact.

Cork was seated now. His hands rested on the table, solid and real. The rabbit lay beside him, one paw brushing his wrist.

Across from him sat the man.

Ordinary. Forgettable.

His smile settled easily into place.

"Rest is a gift," the man said. "You've carried enough."

The words pressed close, shaped like kindness.

"You don't have to reach so hard," the man continued. "Truth doesn't need to cost you everything."

Cork's fingers curled into the rabbit's fur.

Something moved.

The man gestured.

His sleeve slid back.

The tattoo was there.

But now it shifted.

The ink rippled. Lines loosened. The closed circle unwound as the serpent stirred, sliding beneath the skin, rising slowly up the man's arm.

Cork stared, frozen.

The man's eyes changed.

Not all at once—first a flicker, then a glow. Red. Ancient.

The voice followed.

Smooth still—but threaded with a hiss, like breath dragged across scales.

“Belonging doesn’t have to ask for surrender,” it said. “Unity is enough.”

Faces around the table blurred. Features softened, melted, pressed together until there were no edges left.

Sameness.

Cork tried to speak.

The rabbit trembled.

The man leaned forward, eyes burning now—the calm slipping at last.

“You’ve already come so far,” the Deceiver whispered. “Why risk losing what you’ve found?”

His voice dropped, intimate and venomous.

“Truth doesn’t have to be so demanding.”

The table split apart.

The world tore open.

Light and darkness collided—not as armies, not as figures—but as forces that crushed the air between them.

Cork was no longer at the table.

He was standing apart.

And before him stood his father.

Dad looked as he had in the waking world—tired, guarded, his shoulders set as if braced against a blow that never quite landed. He stood between pressures he could not see, his hands clenched and unclenched at his sides.

The darkness moved first.

It did not rush.

It circled.

“You’ve carried enough,” the Deceiver said—not to Cork, but to Dad. “You’ve lost enough. You did what you could. No one can ask more than that.”

The red glow pulsed.

“Faith is for people who need answers,” the voice continued. “You survived without them. You kept your son alive. That’s enough.”

The darkness leaned closer.

“Let the boy believe if he must,” it murmured. “But you don’t need to follow him. Truth shouldn’t demand that much.”

Dad’s jaw tightened.

The Light answered.

Not with argument.

With presence.

It surged forward, filling the space between breaths, pressing back the dark without effort or strain.

“Clint,” the voice said.

The name landed like thunder.

"You were not made for fear," the Righteous King spoke. "You were made for truth."

The darkness recoiled, hissing.

"I entered the darkness for you," the Light continued. "Not to erase your questions—but to answer them."

The presence widened, encompassing both of them.

"I do not abandon those who follow Me."

The disc tore free from Cork's pocket.

It rose into the air—not spinning wildly, not blazing—but steady. Alpha. Omega. The triangle gleaming, still waiting.

"This is a witness," the voice said. "Not to force belief—but to reveal truth."

The darkness screamed, unraveling—not struck down, but undone by what it could not withstand.

Cork did not speak.

He did not act.

He stood.

Light flooded the space.

The table vanished.

The fire collapsed into shadow.

The dream cracked apart.

And Cork fell—into waking, the rabbit clutched tight against his chest, the echo of a voice burning into his soul—

Not a command.

A call.

Not an answer.

A warning.

And a choice still unfinished.

Chapter 28
Awakening

Cork woke like he'd been pulled out of deep water.

His eyes snapped open.

For a heartbeat he didn't know where he was—only that the air tasted of stone and smoke that wasn't there, only that something inside him was still running.

The rabbit was in his hands.

He hadn't remembered reaching for it, but there it was, clutched against his chest as if he'd been holding on through the whole night. The fabric was warm from his grip. One ear—always the same ear—was bent beneath his fingers.

Cork's breath came too fast.

His mind tried to steady itself, to stack the pieces in the right order.

The table.

Lantern light.

A voice that sounded kind until it didn't.

Truth doesn't have to be so demanding.

The words hissed again in the space behind his eyes, slick and intimate, as if they belonged there.

Cork swallowed hard.

He shifted, careful not to make the narrow bed creak.

The room was dim, lit only by the faint glow of a lantern in the corridor beyond their door. He turned his head.

Dad was still asleep.

For a moment, Cork just watched him.

Dad lay on his side, one arm folded beneath his head the way he always did when he was exhausted, his face turned toward the wall. In the low light, his features looked older—lines carved deeper by grief and long miles. His breathing was steady.

Safe.

The word rose automatically, the way it had in the hallways and over meals.

But the dream had made the word feel thin.

Cork's fingers slid from the rabbit to his pocket.

The disc was there.

Cork's thumb traced the gear-edged rim, then the raised grooves of the symbols without pulling it free.

Alpha.

Omega.

And the triangle.

A question for later.

Cork's throat tightened.

He could wake Dad.

He could shake him, whisper, tell him everything—tell him about the voice, the eyes, the serpent that had moved beneath skin like it belonged there.

But something in Cork held him back.

Not fear.

Not doubt.

Something quieter.

Dad needed more than warning.

Dad needed truth.

And Cork didn't yet know how to hand someone truth like a thing you could carry.

Not yet.

Cork eased off the bed and slid his feet onto the cold stone floor. The chill climbed into his bones, sharp enough to clear his head.

He stood, rabbit still in one hand, the other pressed to his pocket as if the disc might leave him again.

The dream had not shown him everything.

It hadn't needed to.

It had shown him enough.

The man.

The mark.

The Oasis.

And the lie.

Cork glanced once more at Dad.

"I'll be right back," he whispered, though he wasn't sure who he was saying it to.

Then he slipped into the corridor.

The Refuge at night was never silent.

Water moved deep beneath the stone, steady as breathing. Lantern flames trembled behind glass as if they could feel the world above, even buried under rock. Somewhere far down the passage, a door clicked shut—careful, deliberate.

Cork moved quickly but quietly.

His bare feet made almost no sound.

He knew the way now. He'd learned the turns and bends over days, learned which corridors led to workrooms and which led to teaching chambers, which ones curved back toward the communal hall.

Deborah.

If anyone would understand without needing to be convinced, it would be her.

She had been there at the Oasis.

She had seen what Cork had seen.

Maybe she had seen more.

Cork's pace quickened.

The rabbit bounced lightly against his side as he ran. He tightened his grip and pressed it to his chest again, as if holding it close could hold his courage steady too.

He passed a small chamber where two lamps still burned low. A man sat alone at a table, head bent over a slate, symbols scratched in pale lines. He looked up as Cork hurried past, eyes narrowing—not in alarm, but in calculation.

Cork didn't stop.

He rounded another bend.

A low vibration rolled through the stone beneath his feet.

Cork slowed, heart stuttering.

It wasn't loud—not yet—but it carried weight. A deep, distant groan that felt less like sound and more like pressure, as if the mountain itself had shifted and not fully settled back into place.

The walls trembled once, just enough to make the lantern glass shiver.

Cork's pulse spiked.

The dream's warning pressed closer—not words now, but urgency.

He broke into a run.

Ahead, the corridor widened.

Deborah stood there, half turned, speaking urgently to two guards. One hand was already on her pack, the other lifted as if issuing orders faster than the Refuge could respond.

“Deborah!” Cork shouted.

She spun, eyes locking onto him instantly.

“What is it?” she demanded, already moving toward him. “What did you see?”

Cork skidded to a stop in front of her, breath tearing at his chest.

“The spy from the Oasis is—”

The world broke.

Stone screamed.

The side wall exploded inward as rock and debris tore through the corridor in a violent roar. The ground bucked beneath Cork’s feet. Air punched from his lungs as he was thrown backward, the rabbit ripped from his grasp as dust and darkness swallowed everything.

Shouts vanished into thunder.

Light vanished.

The Refuge shook.

Chapter 29

Flight to the Inner Refuge

The bells began like an argument between metal and stone.

Hard. Sharp. Unrelenting.

Their sound cut through the Refuge, bouncing off corridor walls and tearing into every chamber as if the mountain itself had learned to scream.

Cork came to with grit in his mouth.

He lay on his back on cold stone, the air thick with dust that stung his eyes and turned every breath into a scrape. For a moment he couldn't remember where he was—or what had happened—only that his ears rang and the world tilted.

Bodies surged past him.

Boots. Bare feet. Cloaks dragging. A child crying somewhere close enough to be heard but not close enough to be seen.

"Move!" someone shouted.

"Inner Refuge! Now!"
"Where's my son—?"

The voices blurred into one rushing river.

Cork pushed up on his elbows.

Pain flashed along his ribs and into his shoulder. He tasted blood and dust, and when he coughed, it felt like the mountain coughed with him.

Something soft brushed his hand.

The rabbit.

It lay half buried in dust a few inches away, one ear bent beneath a layer of pale grit. Cork snatched it up so fast his fingers shook. He pressed it to his chest, as if it could anchor him.

The bell's clang struck again.

Cork's mind snapped into order.

Deborah.
The corridor.
His own voice—The spy from the Oasis is—

Then the wall breaking.

Cork staggered to his feet.

The hallway ahead was half-lit, half-dark. Lanterns swung wildly on hooks, their flames snapping sideways with each tremor, throwing shadows across stone like living things. Dust drifted in sheets. Somewhere above, small rocks pattered down like rain.

A guard shoved past him.

"Don't stop!" the guard barked. "Keep moving!"

Cork turned in the direction the crowd flowed—toward the Inner Refuge.

People pressed shoulder to shoulder now, streaming down the corridor in a frantic line. Some held children. Some carried bundles. Most carried nothing but fear.

Cork took two steps with them.

Then he stopped.

Dad.

Cork twisted, scanning through the smoke and bodies.

"Dad!" he shouted.

His voice vanished under the bells.

A surge of people slammed into him from behind, forcing him forward. Cork braced his feet, fighting to keep his ground.

"Go!" someone yelled at him. "Don't turn back!"

Cork's heart hammered, loud in his ears.

He forced his way sideways, slipping between two panicked adults, ducking under an arm, pushing through the press of bodies as if swimming upstream.

"Dad!" he shouted again.

This time, he heard something.

Not words.

Just a familiar steadiness in the chaos—his father's voice somewhere ahead, calling directions, grounded even when everything else broke.

Cork lurched toward it.

The corridor narrowed.

Smoke thickened, turning lantern light into a weak glow. The Refuge felt suddenly unfamiliar, as if the paths he'd learned had shifted under pressure.

Another tremor rolled through the stone.

A scream rose.

Then—through the haze—Cork saw her.

Deborah.

She was on one knee near a fractured doorway, one hand pressed to her side. Dust streaked her face. Her cloak was torn at the hem. A guard had his arm under hers, trying to haul her upright.

Deborah's head snapped up.

Her eyes found Cork immediately.

"Deborah!" Cork stumbled toward her.

She opened her mouth—then the corridor jumped again as stone groaned under stress.

Deborah winced, gripping the guard's arm. She lifted her free hand and pointed down the corridor with fierce insistence.

"Inner Refuge!" she shouted. "Now—Cork, go!"

Cork's feet locked.

He wanted to tell her.

The spy.
The mark.
The lie.

But the guard was already pulling Deborah back into the shadows of another passage.

Cork took a step after her.

Deborah shook her head once—sharp and final.

Go.

Cork swallowed.

He turned.

And ran.

The crowd carried him at first, sweeping him forward through a corridor that shook with each distant impact. The bells rang in waves now, joined by shouts that sharpened into commands.

"Keep moving!"
"Don't stop!"
"Children to the center—hold on to the one in front of you!"

Smoke burned Cork's eyes. He wiped his face with the back of his wrist, the rabbit pinned tight against his ribs.

Then he heard it again.

"Cork!"

The sound cut through everything.

Cork spun.

Dad was behind him—running.

Not far.

Dad's shirt was smeared with dust, his hair wild, his face set in the hard focus Cork recognized from the canyon and the road—his father in motion, protecting even as he fled. Dad steadied a stumbling woman with one hand, then released her when she found her footing.

Their eyes locked.

For a moment, the bells faded.

The corridor narrowed into only one thing: Dad's face.

"Cork!" Dad shouted again, fierce with love and urgency. "Get to safety! I'm right behind you! I'll meet you there!"

Cork's feet moved.

He ran.

Dad ran too.

Cork glanced back as he pushed forward, counting the distance without meaning to.

Fifty yards.
Thirty.
Dad was gaining.
Twenty.

A new surge of bodies crashed into Cork from behind, forcing him faster.

The Inner Refuge entrance loomed ahead—a wide opening reinforced with carved stone supports, guards posted on either side shouting people through.

"Inside! Inside! Don't stop!"

Cork stumbled as the press tightened.

He heard Dad behind him, close enough now that Cork could feel his voice more than hear it.

“I’m here,” Dad called. “I’m right—”

Cork crossed the threshold.

The air changed.

Cooler.
Heavier.

As if the Inner Refuge held its own breath.

The crowd pushed him deeper, away from the entrance.

Then a sound slammed through the Refuge like a fist.

A deep, final boom.

Stone grinding into stone.

Cork spun.

Where the opening had been, there was only rock.

Not a door.
Not a gate.

A solid wall—seamless, unforgiving, as if the mountain itself had decided to close its mouth.

Cork’s breath caught.

“No—!”

He ran back toward the wall, shoving past people as they stumbled in. He slammed his hands against the stone.

“Dad!” he shouted. “Dad!”

His voice came back small against the rock.

Others pressed near, pounding too.

"Open it!" someone screamed.
"My child is out there!"
"Please!"

Guards rushed in, forming a line.

One of them grabbed Cork's shoulders.

"Stop!" the guard ordered.

Cork shoved at him. "My dad's out there!" Cork's voice cracked. "He was right behind me—he was right there!"

The guard's grip tightened.

His eyes were wide, not cold.

"I know," he said, voice rough. "I know."

"Open it!" Cork pleaded.

The guard shook his head once.

"If we open it," he said, "we lose everyone inside."

The words didn't make sense.

How could safety mean leaving people?

How could refuge mean shutting a father out?

Cork's chest heaved.

He pressed his forehead to the stone wall, as if he could hear through it.

Nothing.

Only distant chaos fading somewhere beyond.

The bells still rang, but softer now—like they were far away.

Cork clutched the rabbit until his fingers ached.

He wanted to run.
He wanted to dig through the wall.
He wanted to wake up.

But the stone did not move.

And the Inner Refuge—packed with breath, fear, and trembling silence—settled around him.

Dad was not there.

And for the first time since the dream, Cork understood what the Deceiver had meant when it whispered:

You will stand alone.

Chapter 30

Where Silence Gathers

Time did not return to the Inner Refuge all at once. It crept back in fragments.

A lantern relit and left burning. A corridor cleared of rubble. A voice lowered from shouting to speaking. Then to whispering. Then to prayer.

Days passed—how many, Cork couldn't have said. The Inner Refuge did not measure time the way the world outside once had. There were no mornings marked by sun or nights marked by stars. There was only the slow settling of people into a space that had saved them and cost them something all at once.

The wounded were brought in first.

Men and women carried on makeshift stretchers.

Children clutched close, eyes too wide for their faces.

Medics moved constantly, hands steady, voices calm, speaking names and instructions with practiced gentleness.

And then—after the first long night—others arrived.

Those who had been trapped in the outer passages. Those who had hidden where the stone had held. Those who had waited in darkness and were finally led through narrow paths into the Inner Refuge.

Each arrival stirred Cork's chest with a hope he did not dare speak aloud.

He watched every face.

Every time the guards escorted a new group through the corridors, Cork straightened. Every time a familiar shape emerged from the dust and dim light, his heart jumped.

Then fell.

Dad did not appear.

Cork moved through the Inner Refuge like someone walking through shallow water—slow, careful, trying not to disturb what little peace had settled.

He searched without rushing.

He checked faces he recognized from meals and lessons. He scanned the medics' areas, careful not to interrupt their work. He asked a guard once, quietly, and received a gentle shake of the head.

He asked Mara.

She was seated near a cluster of women, her hands busy folding clean cloth. When Cork spoke his father's name, she paused, her fingers stilling mid-fold.

"I haven't seen him," she said softly. "But they're still

bringing people in."

Not no.

Not yes.

Just maybe.

Cork nodded and thanked her, even though gratitude felt thin in his throat.

He kept moving.

Whenever someone needed help, Cork stepped in.

He carried water between resting places. He handed clean cloth to medics. He steadied a frightened child whose mother trembled too badly to stand. He gave up his place near the wall so an older man could sit.

Each small act should have eased him.

Instead, they pressed heavier.

The thought returned again and again.

I shouldn't be here.

Dad should be here.

As order slowly returned, leadership gathered names.

Cork waited his turn, rabbit tucked under one arm, fingers worrying its worn ear. When he reached the table, he spoke clearly.

"My father," he said. "Clint Kingson."

The man recording names looked up. "Injured?"

"I don't know," Cork answered.

"Seen entering the Inner Refuge?"

Cork swallowed. "No."

The man nodded and wrote the name down anyway, careful and deliberate.

Cork leaned forward, watching the ink dry, as if staying close might change what it meant.

"Where will he be listed?" Cork asked.

The man hesitated, then turned the page slightly so Cork could see the heading written at the top.

UNCONFIRMED / MISSING

Cork stared at the words.

"They're still searching," the man said gently. "We'll let you know if anything changes."

Cork nodded.

He stepped back.

Nothing changed.

Later, Cork found himself sitting at the sealed stone door—the place where the Refuge had closed between him and his father. His back rested against the cold rock, knees pulled to his chest. The rabbit lay in his lap, its patched seams warm from his hands, the only soft thing left against the stone.

He wasn't crying.

He wasn't praying.

He was just... waiting.

That was where Eli found him.

Eli didn't speak at first. He sat down beside Cork, close enough to be present, far enough not to crowd. The Inner Refuge breathed around them—quiet footsteps, low murmurs, the faint sound of water moving somewhere deep in the mountain.

"When the noise stops," Eli said at last, "the questions get louder."

Cork nodded, eyes fixed on the stone floor.

Eli followed his gaze to the rabbit. "You've been carrying that everywhere."

Cork shrugged. "It helps me remember what's real."

Eli smiled faintly. Not amused. Understanding.

After a moment, Eli rose and nodded down a narrower corridor branching off from the main chamber.

"Walk with me," he said.

They moved slowly, side by side, the noise of the Inner Refuge fading as the passage narrowed. Their footsteps echoed softly, the stone underfoot worn smooth by generations who had passed this way carrying questions they could not name.

Cork broke the silence first. "I keep thinking... if I had moved faster. If I hadn't hesitated."

Eli didn't answer right away. "Obedience doesn't always feel clean," he said at last. "Especially when it costs us something we love."

They walked a little farther.

"There comes a moment," Eli continued quietly, "when

truth is no longer just something we learn about. It becomes something that calls to us."

Cork glanced at him. "Calls how?"

Eli's gaze shifted ahead, thoughtful. "Not with force. Not with fear." He placed a hand briefly over his own chest. "More like a drawing. A stirring. The Breath of the Creator moving a heart toward what is real."

Cork felt it then—a gentle pressure, not from outside but from within, like a steady pull he had been resisting without knowing it.

They stopped.

"The Sanctuary is open," Eli said.

Cork looked up. "For... answers?"

Eli shook his head. "Not only."

"What else?" Cork asked.

"A place to breathe," Eli said. "To be still. To bring fear without pretending you don't have it."

He paused, choosing his words.

"It isn't safety," Eli added. "And it isn't escape."

Cork waited.

"It's stillness," Eli finished. "Especially when faith feels thin."

Cork drew a steady breath.

The entrance to the Sanctuary was simple. No guards. No barriers. Just stone worn smooth by generations of feet that had approached it with hope, fear, or nothing left at all.

Cork stopped at the threshold.

Dad was still missing.
The list still hadn't changed.
Nothing had been resolved.

Cork tightened his grip on the rabbit.

Then he stepped forward.

And entered the Sanctuary alone.

Chapter 31

The Book of Light

The Sanctuary was not empty.

Others were there—scattered along the outer edges of the chamber. Some sat with heads bowed. Some knelt. Some stared ahead with unfocused eyes, as if listening for something they were afraid they might miss. No one spoke. No one moved toward Cork when he entered. No one asked his name.

It was a place open to all.

But not a place anyone entered together.

The air felt different here. Not heavier—clearer. It held a faint hue that was almost imperceptible, a soft blue cast that did not shine so much as *rest* in the space, as if the light itself knew where it belonged. Sounds softened as if the stone itself absorbed them. Cork became aware of his breathing, the faint creak of leather beneath his boots, the quiet scrape of the rabbit's worn fabric as he shifted it in his hand.

He stood there longer than he meant to.

No one told him where to go.

And yet, he knew.

The same gentle pull he had felt in the corridor with Eli stirred again—not urgent, not insistent. Just steady. Certain. It did not command him forward. It invited him.

A thought surfaced that did not feel like his own, yet did not feel foreign either—quiet, patient, nearer than breath:

Come.

Cork drew a slow breath and began to walk.

Near the entrance, a single lantern rested in an iron cradle, its flame low but steady. Cork paused just long enough to lift it free, feeling the familiar warmth settle into his palm before he moved on.

He passed others who did not look up. Each seemed wrapped in their own unseen struggle, their own silent wrestling. Some trembled. Some wept without sound. Some sat rigid, as if afraid that moving would cost them something they were not ready to give.

Cork realized then that whatever waited ahead was not reserved for him alone.

But the path was his to walk.

The chamber narrowed as he moved forward, the ceiling lowering slightly, the stone walls closing in. His lantern cast a small circle of light ahead of him, its flame steady in his left hand. The rabbit rested in his right—its patched seams familiar beneath his fingers, its weight grounding him.

The pull strengthened—not faster, not louder, but clearer.

Do you trust Me enough to take another step? the Breath seemed to ask.

Cork hesitated.

Images pressed in on him—his father's back disappearing through the crowd, the sound of stone sealing shut, the empty space beside him where his dad should have been. Fear tightened his chest.

"I don't know where this leads," Cork whispered.

The stillness did not argue.

You do not need to know, came the answer. *Only whether you will come.*

Cork swallowed and took another step.

The Breath did not praise him. It did not rush him. It waited.

What are you holding that you are afraid to release?

Cork's grip tightened instinctively around the rabbit.

"My dad," he said quietly. "I don't want to believe if it means losing him."

The stillness remained, gentle and unyielding.

Belief does not decide what you lose, the Breath answered. *It decides whom you trust when you cannot keep what you love.*

Cork felt the truth of it settle—not like comfort, but like clarity.

He walked until the pull led him no farther.

He stopped.

Before him, the stone wall was unbroken. There was no door. No arch. No visible passage.

This was the place of decision.

"I don't know everything," Cork said quietly.

The words felt small in the stillness.

"I don't even know most things," he went on. "I don't know what will happen. Or if my dad is alive. Or why the world broke the way it did."

His grip tightened on the rabbit.

"But I know this," Cork said. "I believe the truth matters. Even when it costs. Even when it hurts."

Silence stretched.

Not empty.

Waiting.

Cork drew a steady breath. "I believe," he said.

The Disc stirred.

Warmth spread through his pocket, not burning, not sharp—just present. Cork reached inside and drew it out. The gold caught the lantern light, its gear-edged rim glinting softly. For a moment, it hovered between his hands, lighter than it should have been.

Stone shifted.

Not violently. Not suddenly.

A seam appeared where there had been none before. The wall parted just enough to reveal a narrow passage descending beyond sight.

The Breath fell silent.

Its work was done.

Cork did not look back.

But as he stepped forward, his fingers closed around the Disc once more. He did not understand why—not fully—but he knew it was not finished yet. Not for him alone. He held it quietly, as one holds something meant for another, and then moved on.

He slipped it back into his pocket, not with urgency or reverence, but with care—like something entrusted to him, waiting for the moment it would be needed again.

The passage opened into a chamber carved deeper into the mountain—a cave shaped by intention rather than accident. The stone here was smoother, older, marked not by tools but by time and truth. The same quiet blue light lingered here as well, not emanating from any single source, but present all the same, as if the chamber itself remembered Light. Stone steps rose gently toward a small altar at the far end. Cork climbed slowly, lantern held high in his left hand, the rabbit pressed close in his right.

At the top rested the Book of Light.

It did not glow.

It did not move.

It was ancient and unmarred, its presence steady and unmistakable, as if the stone around it had been formed for no other purpose than to hold it. Cork felt the weight of it before he reached the altar—not physical weight, but meaning.

He stopped a few steps away.

Only then did he notice the folded paper still in his pocket.

Cork drew it out and unfolded it beneath the lantern's light. The words were familiar now, but they struck deeper than before:

The Kingdom is like a treasure hidden in a field.
When a man finds it, he hides it again, returns home, and sells all he has to buy the field.

Cork lowered the paper.

He understood.

Truth would not fit into the life he had before. It would reshape it. Claim it.

He placed the note on the stone near the altar and stepped forward.

The rabbit slipped from his hand next, set carefully at his feet. Cork hesitated, then stepped forward without it, his hands open, empty. Cork raised the lantern higher and opened his hands, palms empty.

"I'm Yours," he said.

The Book opened.

Light spilled forth—not blinding, not harsh, but alive. It filled the chamber with clarity, settling into Cork's bones, steadying his breath, quieting every fear that had shouted at him since the world fell apart.

A voice spoke.

Not loud. Not distant.

Certain.

Cork froze.

He knew the voice.

Not because he had heard it many times—but because he had heard it *once*, and it had marked him.

It was the same voice from the dream. The voice that had driven back the darkness. And yet, beneath it, within it, was the same nearness he had felt earlier—the quiet pull of the Breath that had guided him step by step.

They were not different.

The Breath had been drawing him.

The Voice now named him.

Cork.

He felt the truth of it—not as sound, but as knowing.

You have believed that I am real.

The Light did not rush him.

But belief alone does not bring you out of darkness.

Cork's chest tightened.

You have seen the truth. You have heard it. Now you must choose whether you will leave what binds you to the dark.

Images rose unbidden—fear, self-protection, the quiet bargain to keep his life mostly the same while holding truth at a distance.

To walk in the Light, the voice continued, *you must turn from the darkness.*

Not condemnation.

Invitation.

Cork bowed his head.

“I don’t want the darkness anymore,” he said, voice breaking. “Even the parts I’ve learned to live with.”

The Light deepened.

Then leave it behind.

Cork exhaled—slow, complete.

“I will follow You,” he said. “Not just believe You.”

The Light answered, steady and unyielding.

Then obedience will follow.

Not comfort.
Not certainty.

Only obedience.

Then hear who you are.

Child of the Righteous King.

Cork’s breath caught.

The voice continued, unwavering.

I am the Way, the Truth, and the Life.
There is no other way.
The Creator invites you into the Light of Truth through Me.

The Light did not promise safety.

It promised truth.

Truth that demanded surrender.

Truth that required leaving what was false, even when it felt familiar.

Truth that did not force itself upon him—but would not follow him halfway.

Cork stepped back down the stone steps carrying no book, no lantern, no proof that could be argued.

At the foot of the altar, he paused. He bent, lifted the rabbit gently into his arms, and held it there—not as something he clung to, but as something entrusted to him.

When he emerged from the Sanctuary, he was unchanged to any outward eye.

But he had turned from darkness.

And he walked forward now—not merely believing—but belonging.

A child of the Righteous King.

Chapter 32
After the Light

Cork stepped out of the Sanctuary into the muted calm of the Inner Refuge.

The noise had not returned.

Instead, there was the low, human sound of survival after fear—quiet voices, the shuffle of weary feet, the soft murmur of prayer spoken without ceremony. Some people slept where they sat, heads bowed against stone walls. Others tended bandages or held one another, as if touch itself were proof that the world had not fully broken.

Cork paused just beyond the threshold.

Nothing looked different.

The stone was the same. The lamps burned with the same dim patience. The people carried the same weariness. And yet something in him registered the space differently now—not sharper, not brighter, but *truer*. As if he were no longer searching for where he belonged, but learning how to remain where he stood.

He realized, faintly surprised, that he was not afraid of being seen.

Eli was waiting.

Not standing guard. Not pacing. Simply present, seated on a low stone bench near the entrance, his hands folded loosely as if he had been there for some time. When Cork appeared, Eli rose—not quickly, not urgently—but with intention.

He studied Cork's face for a long moment.

"You stayed," Eli said.

Cork nodded. His throat felt tight, but his voice held.

"I couldn't leave."

Eli searched his eyes, not for answers, but for truth. Whatever he saw there made his shoulders ease, as if something he had been carrying quietly could now be set down.

After a breath, Cork said the words—not loudly, not carefully rehearsed.

"I chose the Light."

Eli closed his eyes for a brief moment, as if receiving something precious. When he opened them again, his gaze was steady.

"Then it has you now," he said.

No celebration followed.
No questions.
Only understanding.

Cork moved deeper into the Inner Refuge.

People made space for him without realizing they were doing it. He noticed how easily his steps found their way, how his eyes were drawn not to the loudest need but to the quietest ones—the child sitting too still, the man gripping his own hands as if afraid they might shake apart.

He passed a woman offering water from a chipped cup and took it from her, pressing it into another's hands without thinking. He steadied a young boy whose leg was wrapped too tightly, loosening the cloth with careful fingers. He knelt beside an older man shaking with exhaustion and waited until the tremor passed.

Only later did he realize how natural it felt.

The movement did not come from guilt or fear.
It rose from the same quiet pull he had felt in the Sanctuary—a steady urging toward compassion.

The Breath did not ask him to explain the Light.
It asked him to love.

For the first time since the world had broken, Cork felt useful in a way that did not depend on survival alone. He was not fixing what was shattered. He was simply *present* within it. And somehow, that was enough.

Mara saw him before he reached her.

She crossed the space between them quickly and pulled him into her arms. The hug was firm, grounding, the kind that did not ask permission. Cork's face pressed into her shoulder, and for a moment he did not try to pull away.

When she finally loosened her grip, she held him at arm's length and searched his face.

"You've seen something," she said.

Cork swallowed. "Someone."

Mara nodded once. She did not ask more.

Her hands stayed on his shoulders.

For a moment, she only looked at him. Her eyes glistened, as if something deep within her had been stirred—hope and grief crossing paths too closely to be separated. She blinked once, and Cork saw the tears gather there, held back by effort alone.

Then her expression changed.

Not suddenly.
Not dramatically.
Just enough for Cork to feel it before she spoke.

"Cork..." she said quietly. "They found your father."

The words landed like stone.

Cork did not ask where.
Or how.
He did not wait for the rest of the sentence.

"He's dead," he said.

The certainty in his voice surprised even him.

Mara shook her head.

"No."

Cork's breath caught.

"But he's barely holding on," she continued, her voice low and steady. "The healers say his body is broken. They've done everything they can."

Her grip tightened, anchoring him.

"If he lives," Mara said, "it will only be because the Creator intervenes."

The words did not soften the fear.
They sharpened it.

Cork nodded once, the rabbit pressed close against his chest without him realizing it. The Disc felt heavy in his pocket now—not warm, not reassuring—just present.

He had chosen the Light.

And now the Light was asking him to stand inside something he could not fix.

Mara turned, guiding him gently toward the infirmary.

Cork followed.

Obedient—not because he understood what would come next, but because he trusted whom he had followed.

And he walked forward, carrying hope as fragile as breath, toward whatever waited on the other side of the stone.

Cork's breath caught.

Chapter 33
What Only the Creator Can Do

The infirmary carried the weight of waiting.

Not urgency. Not panic. But the kind of stillness that settles when all that can be done has already been done, and what remains is no longer in human hands. Lamps burned low along the stone walls, their light steady and warm, casting soft shadows across pallets arranged in careful rows. Healers moved slowly, deliberately, as if haste itself might do harm.

Mara stopped at the edge of the room.

"He's there," she said softly.

Cork stepped forward alone.

Dad lay on a narrow bed of stone and padding, his body wrapped in layers of cloth. One arm was bound tightly to his side, splinted and immobilized. The other rested unnaturally still, the fingers slack. Dark bruising climbed along his jaw and down his neck, fading into bandages that crossed his chest. Each breath came shallow and uneven, as though his lungs had forgotten the rhythm they were meant to keep.

A healer knelt nearby, adjusting a wrap at Dad's ribs. She glanced up when Cork approached and gave a small, tired nod.

"The damage was severe," she said quietly. "Crush injuries. Internal bleeding we've managed to slow, but not stop." She hesitated, choosing her words carefully. "He hasn't woken since he was brought in."

Cork nodded, though the words barely reached him.

The healer rose and took a step away, then paused. She glanced back once, her face softening.

"There are wounds we can bind," she said gently. "And wounds we can only tend." She hesitated, then added, quieter still, "Only the Creator can bring the kind of healing your father needs now."

She bowed her head briefly and moved away, leaving space where only Cork remained.

He pulled a low stool closer and sat beside the bed.

For a long moment, he just looked at his father.

Dad's face was drawn, older than Cork remembered—lines deepened by pain, lips pale, eyes closed beneath dark shadows. This was not the man who had pulled him to safety, who had carried him through fire and fear, who had stood between him and the darkness every step of the way.

"Dad," Cork said quietly.

There was no response.

He swallowed.

“I don’t know if you can hear me,” he went on, his voice low and steady. “But I need to talk anyway.”

He reached out and rested his hand carefully against his father’s, avoiding the bandages.

“I went into the Sanctuary,” Cork said. “I didn’t mean to stay so long. I just... couldn’t leave.”

His chest tightened.

“There’s a Book there,” he continued. “The Book of Light. It isn’t just words. It’s Him. The Righteous King.”

He paused, searching for language simple enough to be true.

“I chose Him,” Cork said. “Not because everything made sense. But because I didn’t want to keep walking in the dark.”

Dad’s breathing stuttered once, then steadied again.

Cork leaned closer.

“I wish I could tell you all of it,” he whispered. “I wish you could see what I saw. Hear what I heard.” His voice faltered. “I wish I could give it to you.”

He fell silent, the weight of helplessness settling in.

Slowly, Cork bowed his head. His shoulders began to shake, the sound of his breath breaking apart as the tears finally came. He did not try to stop them.

“Creator,” he prayed, not loudly, not carefully. “They say only You can save him now.”

He tightened his grip on his father's hand.

"I don't know how You work," Cork said. "And I don't know what You'll choose to do. But I know You're good."

Tears blurred his vision, but he did not look away.

"Please," he whispered. "If it's possible... let him live. Let him wake up. Let him find the Light too."

The room remained still.

No voice answered.

No miracle came.

Cork stayed.

He stayed beside his father, holding hope as gently as he held his hand, trusting the One who gives life—whether by breath, or by waiting.

And there, in the quiet of the infirmary, Cork learned what it meant to believe without seeing.

He did not know if dawn would bring life or loss.

He did not know if this faith would save his father—or cost him everything else.

But Cork stayed.

And in the waiting, the story did not end. It only began to open.

For readers who wish to linger in the world of Cork a little longer, an original cinematic soundtrack inspired by this story is available on major music platforms.

Search:
The Chronicles of CORK: The Quest for the Book of Light (Original Cinematic Soundtrack)

Author's Note

This story was written for those who are still asking questions.

Cork's world is made up, but the things he faces are real—fear, loss, courage, and the hope that light is stronger than darkness. Sometimes life breaks in ways we don't understand, and we are left choosing what to trust next.

In this story, the Light is not just an idea. It is a Person. Someone who enters darkness instead of running from it.

Someone who invites rather than forces.

Someone who asks us to follow, even when we don't see the whole path.

I believe that same Light is real in our world.

He is the One who made us, the One who came to rescue us, and the One who calls us by name. He doesn't promise an easy road—but He does promise to walk it with us.

If this story made you wonder about truth, or hope, or what it means to belong, I hope you keep asking. If you felt drawn toward the Light, I hope you keep walking toward Him.

This is not the end of Cork's journey.

And it doesn't have to be the end of yours either.

About the Authors

Aaron McBride and Alton McBride are a father and son who share a love for stories, imagination, and meaningful adventure. *The Quest for the Book of Light* began years ago as a story Aaron started writing for his children and was later brought to life through a shared journey of creativity with Alton.

Aaron enjoys telling stories that explore faith, courage, and the cost of choosing what is right. Alton brings a sense of wonder, curiosity, and imagination shaped by the perspective of a twelve-year-old, helping ensure the story speaks authentically to readers his age.

They believe stories are meant to be shared—and that the best ones are passed from one generation to the next.

www.ingramcontent.com/pod-product-compliance
Lightning Source LLC
La Vergne TN
LVHW040222110826
845146LV00004B/1256